Modern Stories of Ancient Greece

Chosen and edited by
EDNA COWIN
GEOFFREY FALLOWS
HELEN PAUL and
JOHN SHARWOOD SMITH

LONGMANS

LONGMANS, GREEN AND CO LTD
London and Harlow

*Associated companies, branches and representatives
throughout the world*

© *Longmans, Green and Co Ltd 1969*
First published 1969

SBN 582 34311 9

*Printed in Great Britain by
Western Printing Services Ltd*

In preparation
MODERN STORIES OF ANCIENT ROME

Contents

Contents

Acknowledgements

We are grateful to the following for permission to reproduce copyright material:

The Bodley Head for extracts from *Jason* by Henry Treece, *Oedipus* by Henry Treece and *Electra* by Henry Treece; Chatto & Windus Ltd for an extract from *The Sybil* by Pär Lagerkvist, translated by Naomi Walford; Christy & Moore Ltd for an extract from *Olympic Runner* by I. O. Evans; Faber & Faber Ltd for an extract from *Elephants and Castles* by Alfred Duggan; Rupert Hart-Davis Ltd for an extract from *Alexander the God* by Maurice Druon; Little, Brown & Co. for an extract from *The Torch* by Wilder Penfield, Copyright © 1960, by Wilder Penfield; Longmans Green & Co. Ltd for an extract from *The King Must Die* by Mary Renault and for two extracts from *The Mask of Apollo* by Mary Renault; Max Parrish Ltd for an extract from *Ten Thousand Heroes* by James Barbary; John Murray Ltd for an extract from *Achilles His Armour* by Peter Green; Alvin Redman Ltd for two extracts from *The Golden Lyre* by Noel Gerson; Trade Delegation of the U.S.S.R. in the United Kingdom for an extract from *Land of Foam* by Ivan Yefremov.

The authors would also like to mention their gratitude to Mrs Thelma Bristow who gave them the idea.

Preface

A hundred years ago to be educated meant, for most people, to learn Latin and Greek, and so to know most of the stories, true and legendary, about the Greeks and Romans. Nowadays, with such a vast amount of scientific knowledge and so many new subjects to be studied at school, very few of the hundreds of thousands who go to secondary schools learn much Latin or any Greek at all. The four of us who prepared this book are unusual in having what might now be considered an old-fashioned education. We spent much of our school time and all of our university course studying Latin and the Romans, and Greek and the Greeks. When we talked about it together we found that we had no regrets about being old-fashioned in this way. We certainly wouldn't want anyone to have this sort of education forced on them, as used to happen, and we realize how important it is that everyone should know some science and that some people should know a great deal of one science or other, but we would be sorry if there came a time when *no one* learnt about the Greeks and Romans. Why? Well this is what we find very hard to put into words, except to say that they were fascinating peoples and we feel that in studying them we learnt things about human nature that we couldn't have learnt in any other way. But to explain to anyone *how* they were fascinating we found almost impossible; and to suggest to someone that they should go to the trouble of learning Latin and Greek (neither of them easy languages to learn) just on the chance that they too would find the Greeks and Romans fascinating, is rather preposterous. So we took up a suggestion that we should read through a lot of novels, written by people who are alive today, which deal with Ancient Greece (we are now doing the same for Ancient Rome), to see if we couldn't find a short passage which would arouse the interest of people like yourselves. We each took a number of novels and we met once a month and took it in turns to read out passages we had chosen. Sometimes we voted them out, but mostly we voted them in, and these are the ones you will find in this book. We wrote introductions to all the passages we had chosen, so that it would be possible for you to understand them without having read the rest of the book from which they were taken.

What we hope is that you will enjoy reading the passages and that some of you will want to spend more time studying the Greeks and Romans, and just occasionally one or two of you will be so interested that you will even want to learn Latin or Greek or both.

JOHN SHARWOOD SMITH

Introduction

Some people write stories about the future—science fiction—which is fun because nobody knows what life will be like in the future, and all kinds of possibilities can be imagined, exciting, romantic, amusing, frightening or fantastic; and on the whole the authors who write the best stories are those who know a little about the scientific possibilities of the universe, but not too much. Other people like to write about the past because, although, thanks to historians, to archaeologists and to scholars who can read dead languages, we know something about the past—a lot about some periods, next to nothing about others—nobody really knows what it was like to be a duellist at the court of Louis XIII, or a Viking with a blood feud to carry on, or a Food Taster in the palace of the Emperor Nero. And again the authors who do it best are usually those who know something about the period in which they place their characters but not so much that their imaginations cannot do a lot of work.

The stories in this book, as you will have gathered from the title, are about Greece and Greeks. The great advantage with the Greeks, from the point of view of a storyteller, is that you can choose a very early period in Greek history, and then there will be no written records of it; only elaborate legends, terrifying, grotesque or just romantic and exciting, which were told, and eventually written down, by the Greeks themselves: or you can choose a later period about which quite a lot is known, such as events in the lives of men and women whose character and appearance have been described by writers who knew them, or disasters which befell armies or cities and were narrated from accounts by eyewitnesses. And what everyone knows who has visited Greece or read any books about the Greeks, is that Greece is a very beautiful and exciting country—exciting because of so many mountain passes suitable for ambushes or gallant rearguard actions, so many citadels perched on impregnable rocks, and a sea which can be blue, clear and glassy or ugly and dangerous, even in the short stretches between the scattered islands of the Aegean Sea, and which cuts the coastline into innumerable rocky bays and gulfs. The Greeks were adventurous and quick-witted, fond of fighting and fond of cultivating both their intelligence and the strength and agility of their bodies. They built cunning fortresses and beautiful temples and slim, fast warships; they enjoyed life, but were ready to risk death for their city, and when they killed each other in battle they did so face to face, with the thrust of a spear or sword. Furthermore life among the Greeks was seldom dull. A woman could be a princess, or a man an important citizen, one day and a slave the next. Cities were built, grew beautiful and prosperous and were razed to the ground within a few generations: and these cities were small enough for everyone to know everyone else. Every man, whether he were poet, architect, businessman or politician was also at sometime a soldier, or fighting sailor. Above all it was a proud and precarious thing to be a Greek. Savage tribes menaced you and your city from outside Greece and even within the borders of Greece itself, while the powerful and wealthy Persian Empire for three centuries threatened and intrigued, and held captive Greek cities on the other side of the sea, and had to be fought off from the mainland in two great struggles. When Alexander and his Macedonian armies had conquered Greece as well as Persia his generals, after his death, founded kingdoms (one of which included Greece itself) more like smaller versions of the former Persian Empire than the little city states in which the Greeks had lived until then. The generals became kings and built cities all over Asia Minor and brought Greeks to live in them and fought each other with huge armies of hired soldiers. Life then was exciting for the adventurous, and exciting for everyone—too exciting often— when your city was besieged in one of these wars, but generally more humdrum than in the past, and more like life today.

PART I: THE HEROIC AGE

All that we know about the Heroic Age comes from the archaeologists who have dug up some fifty fortresses and palaces and one great city (Troy), and from the Iliad and Odyssey of Homer, which are themselves a kind of historical novel, being connected stories about the dimly remembered past, written several hundreds of years later. Apart from these sources many stories were handed down which were not incorporated into the Iliad and Odyssey, but were used much later as the plots of plays, or subjects of poems, or simply collected and retold as our fairy stories are. Of all the stories those about the island of Crete are perhaps the most fascinating. By the time the Greeks started to want to write true history the great palaces of Crete were no more than magnificent and mysterious ruins; but seven centuries earlier Cretan kings had commanded great navies and lived in luxury and magnificence, their subjects had worn beautiful jewellery and elaborate dresses, and had indulged in forgotten religious and social customs, which included some form of bull-baiting. All this was dimly remembered long after the power and civilization of Crete collapsed as the result of civil war, invasion, famine or earthquake—no one can be sure which. Never again did the Greeks build such magnificent palaces or revive the sport of bull-baiting, and the story of Theseus, the Minotaur and the Labyrinth were legends which attempted to account for what was remembered of them. A modern writer, Mary Renault, has made her own attempt to guess how the bull-baiting might have taken place and how the palace was destroyed. Another modern writer, Henry Treece, has retold the story of Jason and the Argonauts and their voyage of adventure, which was perhaps created out of confused stories about exploration in the scarcely known waters of the Black Sea (and into the story perhaps there crept other tales, of voyages in the Adriatic—so confused is the geography). The incident of the Clashing Rocks (our second story) possibly recalls the difficulties of making the passage through the Dardanelles. Another story Henry Treece has retold is that of Oedipus, which is so strange and so puzzling that the name of Oedipus is as familiar to students of modern psychology as it is to students of literature. The third story by Henry Treece to appear in this book is that of the return of King Agamemnon from the sack of Troy.

PART II: THE CLASSICAL PERIOD

This includes the sixth, fifth and fourth centuries B.C., when the Greeks had taken to living in cities and were busy making life beautiful and enjoyable with music, dancing and the visual arts—carving statues, building temples, writing plays and creating democracies, and a few of them spending their lives in developing rational philosophy and the beginnings of scientific enquiry. *The Torch*, by Wilder Penfield, tells the life of Hippocrates, the founder of Greek scientific medicine. *The Land of Foam* by Ivan Yefremov is an unusual book. It is difficult to be sure when the events are supposed to take place, and it is about a Greek, but not about Greece. The hero wishing to become a sculptor wanders to Egypt to study the Egyptians' skill in carving, but is enslaved by the Egyptians and put to work in a desert quarry. Yefremov is a Russian and it is difficult not to believe that he has in mind the conditions in some of Stalin's (or possibly Hitler's) concentration camps—but no one can say that it may not have been very similar to be a prisoner of the Egyptians. *Olympic Runner* by M. I. Evans gives a picture of the Greeks' love of athletics, and another story by Mary Renault, *The Golden Mask*, tells of an actor whose life was spent in playing the parts created by writers of tragedies, some of which have survived twenty-five centuries and still move audiences to tears today.

Our other stories of this period are mainly concerned with characters who are well known to us from works of history written by the Greeks themselves. Alcibiades had all the gifts that life can bestow—wealth, good looks, strength, courage and the gift of leadership in peace or war—and yet used these gifts for the destruction of himself and his own city. Xenophon, like many modern generals, did his best to ensure fame by writing a very readable account of his own exploits and those of his companions. About Philip the Great of Macedon we know a great deal both from his friends and his enemies, while his son, Alexander the Great, took an official historian with him to record his deeds.

PART III: THE HELLENISTIC AGE

From this period we have only two stories. In *Elephants and Castles* Alfred Duggan has related the life of one of the most brilliant and adventurous of the many adventurous generals who kept Greece and the Greeks (who were now the ruling class in the lands which Alexander had conquered) in a constant state of warfare. *The Sybil*, by Pär Lagerkvist, is the most powerful and striking of all the novels we read, and more than any of them deserves to be read in full. It describes an aspect of Greek religion – divine prophesy – at a time when the old religious beliefs had begun to wane and priests were often cynical and corrupt. The novel touches on the story of Christ and the legend of the Wandering Jew, and thus reminds us that the Hellenistic period leads up to the rise of Rome as an imperial power, and to the early beginnings of Christianity.

The Bull Baiting

The following excerpt gives Mary Renault's idea of what Cretan bull-baiting was like. The story is told by Theseus, who believed himself to be the son of Poseidon, the God of the Sea and of earthquakes, but who was accepted by the Athenians as the son and heir of their King. Every nine years the Athenians had to send a tribute of seven girls and seven boys to die in the bull-ring and Theseus had volunteered to be one of them. The tribute was imposed by Minos, King of Crete, in recompense for his son who had been accidentally killed at Athens; and Theseus was determined to put an end to the power of Crete over Athens. This he eventually succeeded in doing, with the help of an earthquake sent by his father Poseidon; but first he had to learn how to survive in the bull-ring, before he could organize a revolt of the bull-baiters and of the Cretan peasantry against the lords of the palace. The following passage tells how after long and arduous training he, and the Athenians who had been sent with him, were allowed their first sight of what went on in the bull-ring, and what happened to another team of bull-baiters who were performing that day.

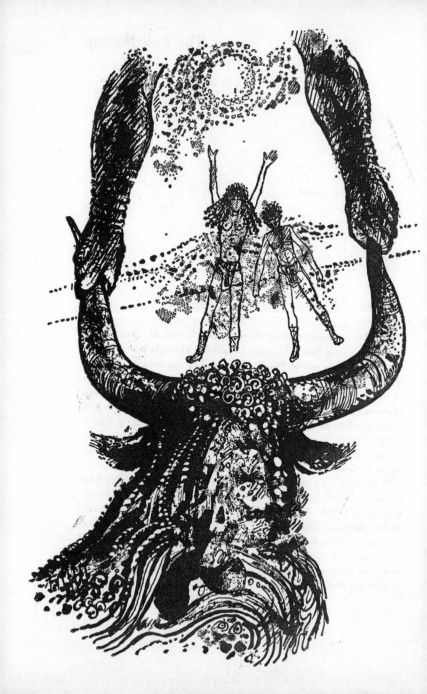

The Bull Baiting

The bull ring stood on the plain east of the Palace. It was built of wood, for Crete is a land of timber. The bull-dancers had their own gallery, just over the dancers' door, and facing the bull gate. It faced the King's box too, but it was a long time, people said, since Minos had seen the Bull Dance. The chief priest of Poseidon hallowed the bull. For the rest, the rite is ruled by the Goddess-on-Earth.

In the chief place of the ring stood a gilded shrine, upheld by crimson pillars and crowned with the sacred horns. On either side were seats for the priestesses, and all round sat the Palace ladies. As we sat down they were coming in from their litters, their slaves spreading cloths and cushions for them to sit on, and giving them their fans. Friends greeted friends, and kissed and called for their seats to be moved together; soon it was like a spreading tree in which a flock of bright birds has settled, cooing and twittering and preening. Massed like dark leaves, the little russet Cretans filled the upper tiers.

Horns blew, a door opened behind the shrine. There she stood. Her foot-high diadem was crested with a golden leopard. If she had not moved, I should have taken her for jeweller's work.

The men all stood, laying fist on breast; the women touched their foreheads. She took her tall throne. There was a music of harps and flutes.

The bull-dancers came in from the door below us. They stepped slowly but lightly, two by two, a girl and a boy, in a solemn dance-step. Their love-locks sleeked and combed bounced on their smooth shoulders, their arm-rings and neck-laces caught the light; the girls' young breasts, and the rumps of their little loin-guards, jigged prettily in the dance. They all had their hands and wrists strapped round to strengthen their grip; boots of soft leather were laced up to their calves. In the first couple was the Corinthian, blithe as a bird.

They circled the ring, and fetched up in one row before the shrine, with the Corinthian in the middle. There they all stood, and made the sign of homage, and spoke a phrase in old Cretan. I tapped the shoulder of the dancer who sat in front of me, and asked, 'What do they say?' She was a black girl from Libya, and had not very much Greek. She said slowly, thinking it out as she spoke, 'Hail, Goddess! We salute you we who are going to die. Receive the offering.'

I looked up at the shrine. She had sat down again, and once more was still, as if made of gold and ivory.

The dancers had turned, and strung themselves in a circle round the ring. A trumpet sounded. In the wall facing us the great bull-gate opened, and out came the bull.

He was a kingly beast, white spatchcocked with brown; thick-barrelled, short-legged, wide-browed, and, like all his breed, very long-horned. The horns curved upward and for-ward, then dipped and rose again at the tips. They were painted lengthwise with stripes of red and gold.

The Corinthian stood facing him across the ring, with his back to us. I saw him lift his hand, saluting; a noble gesture, graceful and brave. Then the dancers began to move around

4

the bull, turning in a circle as the stars do round the earth; far-off at first but getting nearer. At first he did not take much notice; but you could see his big staring eye following them around. He switched his tail, and his feet fidgeted.

The music quickened; and the dancers closed in. They swooped round the bull like a flight of swallows, nearer and nearer. He put his head down, and his forefoot raked the ground. Then you saw what a fool he was. As each dancer flew past his head, he would look, and get ready with a lumbering scrape of his feet, and then say to himself 'Too late', and look sheepish and start again. Now the dancers slowed their spinning, and started to play the bull. First one and then another would pause till they had drawn him, then skim or sway out of his path and leave him for the next. The more daring the dancers are, the more they work the bull, the better for them in the end. He is the stronger; but he is one to their fourteen. He may tire first, if they keep him at it.

So it went on, till the first edge was off him, and he seemed to say, 'After all, who is paying me for this?' Then the Corinthian ran round to face him, and held out both arms; and the circling stopped.

He ran smoothly up to the sullen bull. It was the leap I had seen often in the Bull Court. But that was a shadow; now, he had a living thing to dance with. He grasped the horns, and swung up between them, going with the bull; then he soared free. The beast was too stupid to back and wait for him. It trotted on, when it felt him gone. He turned in air, a curve as lovely as a bent bow's, and on the broad back his slim feet touched down together; then they sprang up again. He seemed not to leap, but to hang about the bull, like a dragon-fly over the reeds, while it ran out from under him. Then he came down to earth, feet still together, and lightly touched the catcher's hands with his, like a civility; he had no need of

steadying. Then he danced away. There was a joyous screaming and cooing from the bird-tree, and shouts from the men.
As for me, I stretched in secret my right hand earthwards,
and whispered under all the noise, 'Father Poseidon! Make
me a bull-leaper!'

The dancers circled again. A girl paused on tiptoe, arms
lifted, palms outspread; an Arabian, the colour of dark honey,
with long black hair. She was straight as a spear, with the
carriage of women used to carry their burdens on their heads;
big disks of gold hung from her ears and threw back the sunlight. Sometimes in the Bull Court I had seen her white teeth
flashing. She was a haughty, mocking girl, but she looked
grave now, and proud.

She grasped the horns, and pressed upward. Perhaps something had been going on in the bull's dull mind; or perhaps her
balance was less true than the Corinthian's. Instead of tossing
up his head, he shook it sideways.

The girl fell across his forehead. Yet she had somehow kept
her hold upon the horns. She hung on them like a monkey,
riding the bull's nose, her feet crossed on his dewlap. He
started to run round and round, shaking his head. I heard a
deep mutter from the men's seats, and from the women's a
high breathless twittering. I looked up at the pillared shrine.
But the golden goddess sat unmoving, and her painted face
was still.

The dancers swooped about, clapping their hands and flip-
ping their fingers to confuse the bull. Yet I thought it was
mostly show and they could have done more. I hammered
with my fist muttering 'Nearer! Nearer!' till the next youth
said to me, 'Keep your hands to yourself, Hellene'; I had been
beating him on the knee. 'He will have her!' I said. 'He is
going to the barrier to beat her off.' The youth muttered, with
his eyes upon the ring, 'Yes, yes; they won't go in for her. She

has been insolent and made enemies.' The bull was trying to find the barrier, but the girl's long hair was in his eyes, and she kept twisting her shoulders to blind him. I said out of breath, 'The Corinthian, can't he help?' He answered leaning foward in his seat, 'It's work for the catcher, not the bull-leaper. Why should he? He never worked with this team before.'

Just as he spoke, the Corinthian leaped forward. He ran at the bull from its left side, and caught the horn and hung on it swinging. The girl, whose strength was finished, dropped off and scrambled to her feet and ran.

Before he jumped, I had seen the Corinthian look swiftly round and beckon. The youth beside me had leaped to his feet and was shouting in his native tongue, which I think was Rhodian; I could tell he was cursing. I was shouting myself. No one can last long as the Corinthian was, unless someone comes up to pull on the other horn. He had counted on that; but no one had done it.

One of the youths came running at last, and made as if to leap and catch the horn. But I could tell it was from shame, and his heart was not in it. So he was too late. The bull swerved from him and put its head down sideways, and scraped off the Corinthian with its foot. Then I saw him rise in the air again; but he soared no longer. He was speared on the horn, which had pierced his midriff, just above the belt. I don't know if he cried out or not. The din was too great to hear. He was tossed and flung down with a great red hole in him. The bull trampled him, then trotted away. The music ceased. The dancers stood still. A deep sigh and murmur ran round the galleries.

They use a little double-axe, of the sacred pattern, to dispatch the victims. When they lifted it over his neck, I saw his hand come up for a moment, as if to ward it off; then he changed the gesture to a salute, and turned his head to take the blow cleaner. He was a gentleman and he died like one. I found myself weeping, as if I had been in love with him. So I was too, though not as it is understood in Crete. No one took notice. To weep once is thought lucky in the Bull Court. Besides, a lady had fallen down screaming, and there was a crowd about her, fanning her and holding essences to her nose and catching her marmoset.

The bull was roped and led away. You could see it was getting tired; it would have had enough before long. The dancers filed out. The Rhodian next me was saying, 'Why did he do it? Why? He had no need.' Then he said, 'I suppose he was called. I suppose it was his time.' I said nothing. My tears had dried; I had begun to think.

The priest of Poseidon had filled a shallow offering-cup with the Corinthian's blood, and poured a libation on the earth. Then he came forward and stood before the shrine, and poured the rest till the cup was empty, and spoke in Cretan. The Mistress in the shrine stood up and raised her palms outward, in the gesture that means 'It is accomplished.' Then she went out through the little door behind the shrine. I remembered the small rouged feet upon the steps, the tender breast with the ringlet on it. My flesh shivered.

When we were back in the Bull Court, I said to Amyntor, 'Fetch the Cranes.'

I waited by the Bull of Daidalos. No one felt like playing with him just then, so we had that place to ourselves. The Cranes came up. I saw Phormion pale, while Amyntor still shook with anger. Of the girls, it was Chryse and These who had been crying; Nephele's eyes were dry. Helike was shut up in one of her silences, and spoke to no one. 'Well,' I said, 'Now we have seen the Bull Dance.'

Amyntor burst out, cursing the team that had let the

Corinthian die. He was a nobleman, and thought of them as a royal guard that has failed its master. I let him run on awhile; he meant it well.

'Yes,' I said. 'But think; he was not of their kin; they owed him nothing; they had sworn him no oath. Why should he have been dearer to them than their lives?'

They looked at me, wondering that I could be so cold.

'On the ship,' I said, 'when I swore us in, it was only to keep us together. I was all ignorance; but I suppose the god prompted me, because I am in his hand. Do you all know now why we must be as kindred?'

They nodded. They were soft metal now, ready for striking. I had been right not to delay.

'The Corinthian is dead,' I said. 'But so are all his team. They gave themselves to death just when they thought to live a little longer. They know it, too. Look at them now. Shame would not weigh so heavy on them. They are afraid.'

'Yes,' said Amyntor. 'That is true.'

'When you love your life too much in the ring, that's when you lose it. Now they are goods no one will buy. They are not worth a graze or a scratch or a trickle of blood to anyone. And they have lost their pride in themselves. If any of them has had a guardian god, they must hear the music of his passing. Look at their faces.'

But instead they all looked at mine, as if I had power to make things other than they were. They thought me hard.

'We are going to renew our oath,' I said, 'so that the gods of this place can witness it. But now we will swear it stronger. 'The life of every Crane shall be as dear to me as mine. What I would look for if I were in his danger, that I will do for him, the very same, not less by a single hair. So witness the River, and the Daughters of Night, and Bull-Faced Poseidon down below Crete. On the day I am forsworn, may they destroy me.'

They looked at me with great eyes. Chryse and Amyntor both stepped forward, in a hurry to repeat the words while they had them right. They had not even looked behind them. I motioned them to wait; I could see the others. Not that I blamed those who hung back; it was a strong oath, and heavy.

'What is it?' I said to them. 'Do you think you are doing it for me? Why should you, indeed? I am a king without a roof of his own, without food or clothes or gold or anything to give, except, like any one of us, whatever I am good for with the bulls. Do this for yourselves. We are only mortal. There will be quarrels among us, love-rivalries, and such things. If you swore there would not, you would be forsworn within a week. But this we can swear, never to bring them into the ring. There we must be limbs of one body, as if we shared one life. We do. We must have no more doubt of each other than the spear-arm has of the shield-arm. Swear to that.'

Then some came forward. I said to the rest, 'Don't be afraid. You will walk lighter after, when there is no looking back. That is a mystery I am telling you. I learned it from a priest who is also a king.'

When all had sworn, there was a silence. Then silly Pylia looked surprised, as if she had gulped strong wine. 'Yes, it is true. I *do* feel better.' We all laughed, more at her face than anything else. But all that day, we found that we were merry.

That night, after the girls had gone, a boy came up to me; a Minyan from Melos, whom I only knew by sight. 'The Corinthian told me,' he said, 'who was to have his things when he met his bull. This is for you.'

He opened his hand. There was a little bull in his palm, of polished crystal. The ring to hang it by was a slender gold bull-leaper, bent in a somersault on its back.

'Me?' I said. 'He hardly knew me.' I did not want the Corinthian to lose his last wish, because of this boy's stupidity. He shrugged his shoulders. 'Oh, it is not a love-gift. Don't flatter yourself. He said he liked to put something on his fancy. Would it be to settle a bet?'

I took it away, and hung it round my neck by a strong thread. I did not reproach myself for having laughed and clowned with the Cranes before his blood was dry. He would have understood that better than anyone.

After dark I went round behind the cook-house. The wicket-gate was ajar as usual. Aktor the trainer, seeing me there, said, 'Which girl tonight? Make the most of her. When you get to the bulls, you'll have less to spare.'

I said something he could laugh at. I was not after a girl that evening. He was right already; the Bull Dance is a jealous mistress. But in the daytime one was never alone.

The Great Court was empty under the moon. Tier upon tier rose the pillared balconies, dimly glowing. Lamps flickered behind curtains of eastern stuff. The pots of lilies and of flowering lemon-trees shed a sweet heavy scent. A cat slipped from shadow to shadow, and a Cretan who looked as if his errand were the same. Then all was silent. The great horns upon the roof-coping reared up as if they would gore the stars.

I stretched out my hands palm downward, and held them over the earth. 'Father Poseidon, Horse Father, Lord of Bulls. I am in your hand, whenever you call me. That is agreed between us. But as you have owned me, give me this one thing first. Make me a bull-leaper.'

The Clashing Rocks

Jason, by Henry Treece, is an account of Jason's life as it might have been told by Jason himself when an old man. He remembers his upbringing by Cheiron the Centaur on Mount Pelion, and his voyage in the ship *Argo* to find the Golden Fleece (a treasure treacherously acquired by the King of Colchis): this he needed to win back his father's kingdom which had been seized by his wicked uncle Pelias. Finally he describes his decline into old age and obscurity.

The following passage is about an encounter of the Argonauts (as the crew of the ship *Argo* were called) with the Clashers, the legendary rocks which crushed ships to pieces as they sailed between them.

The
Clashing
Rocks

Autumn became Winter as our prow pushed onward through the inland sea, the waters ever seeming to thicken, to darken, as we went. Our olive tally-stick became notched from end to end. It was as though we would never reach the place we journeyed to find.

The cold was bitter now, and the land, which we always had in view on our steerboard side, became bare and treeless. At night we slept on shore and foraged where we could, sometimes catching no more than a brace of hares or a few pheasant. Sometimes, at dusk, distant camel trains with their bells tinkling on the cold wind passed us by, but the men who went with them never dared approach our fires, and so we met no one. We felt that the world ignored us, as though we were unclean.

Old Butes came to me as I leaned on the oak prow one afternoon.

'Captain Jason,' he said, looking over his shoulder to see whether anyone was listening to him, 'I am troubled in my mind.'

It was always my custom to let any man of my crew speak

freely to me at all times and so I put my hands on his thin shoulders and said, 'Say on, old fellow. Perhaps I can intercede with the gods for you and rid you of your troubles.'

Butes shook his head. 'My trouble concerns us all,' he answered. 'It is a dream I have each night, a dream so real that this oak staff I hold in my hand is less real than my dream.'

I took his stick and fingered it. 'This seems solid enough to me,' I replied. 'Your dream must be of some consequence.'

He snatched the staff back a little hastily as though he was cross with my mockery. 'Know, Jason,' he said sharply, 'that we have a great trial before us, one that may well cost us our ship and our lives. I dare say no more, for the gods may have given me a secret vision which must not be shared; I do not know. The ways of the gods are not easily interpreted.'

I laughed at him and said, 'Did you seem to see two rocks floating in the waters, waiting to crush us?'

He almost fell and nodded his bald old head so violently that the drip on the end of his sharp red nose fell off.

'By Zeus,' he said, 'so you have this dream also?'

I shook my head and smiled. 'No, old man,' I told him. 'But before we left his palace blind Phineus warned me that all ships must keep an eye open for the Clashers when they have reached these waters. Why else do you think I stand always here at the prow, watching, when I might be under the Captain's awning, warming my hands by the brazier?'

He bowed and went away to his cubby-hole, which we all called the 'beehive', as a taunt to him. He did not row like the other men, being too old and weak in the back.

Three mornings later, we broke through a thick grey mist that lay on the surface of the sea like a wall of smoke. And before us, with the white sea-birds crying above them, were the Clashers, two gigantic pyramids of ice, half blue, half grey, and rearing up so high that the *Argo* seemed like one of those ivory toy-boats that Cretans still carve for their sons in memory of their once-great sea-kingdom.

The men stopped rowing and began to back-water with their broad-bladed oars. For a while there was complete silence as they turned and saw what lay before them. Then the babble broke out, and Atalanta clutched her throat as though she suddenly feared to die, to lose her young life, her hungry body, and to sink in the cold waters for the fishes to eat.

I could not help taunting her. 'Well, sister,' I called out, 'now tell me, does this sea belong to Poseidon or to Aphrodite? If the first, then I shall do what I can to save us. If the second, then I hand over my duties to you. Then you shall make the plans.'

The wretch fell on her numbed knees and held out her hands to me, crying. 'This stretch belongs to Poseidon, Captain,' she said. 'There can be no doubt of it.'

We all laughed then because it was pleasant to see this proud woman on her knees, begging.

I bowed as if accepting my authority from her, though in all truth I must have felt as troubled in my mind as she did, for I had never seen such mountainous blocks of ice before, having come from the warm seas. But it is not a captain's part to show his fears to his crew, so I put on a good face and called out to the men to get up a little more speed.

I had noticed that these two ice-floes swung against each other, rubbing their sides with a great crunching and then swinging apart with some undertow of the tides.

I would have rowed round them, but now I saw that there were others coming southwards, in line, like horsemen entering a city. To go round the Clashers would be to meet the oncoming floes in any case. So I made the men pull *Argo* closer and closer, until at last we lay in the dark icy shadow, right underneath their terrible majesty.

They were very beautiful in their way and must have come a long distance—perhaps as far as we had come—breaking off from the far northern ice-land and floating with the current towards the southern shores. Sea-birds nested on them and Acastus even thought he saw a wolf prowling on a ledge, two masts high, on one of them, as though it had been cut adrift when this floe broke away.

We heard the crunching of ice on ice, a horrible, tearing sound. Pieces fell into the leaden waters with a great splash, drenching us; we were so near.

Three times I watched these two masses rub together and then swing away again, perhaps a ship's width, to loll on the slow tide once more, waiting for the next encounter.

Old Butes cried out, 'The gods guide us, Jason! Have a care! They wait to trap us.'

Castor shouted to him, 'What, old sheep, are you afraid to go into the waters and feed the fishes then? Why, your scraggy old bones would hardly serve as a snack for some of the brisk young fellows whose fins I have seen in the last few days!'

This made us all laugh, and while they were in this frightened merry mood I watched the movement of the ice-floes and then, suddenly, beat my mallet hard on the prow and bawled out, 'Right! Row now for your very lives!'

Ancaeus gripped the steerboard helm as though it had been a bucking stallion, to keep the nose of *Argo* straight. The men rowed so hard that I feared their oars would snap.

As we flew nearer, I felt the ship shudder when our keel crunched on some underlying ledge of ice, below the water. It halted us a little but the men pulled like maniacs after this.

Then we were almost in darkness. It was like going down a narrow street between two high houses where the light never reaches and the sun's heat cannot penetrate. There was no room to row now and we had to ship the oars speedily. I leaned over the side and let my hand run along the ice as we went on with the dying impetus of our last strokes. The walls were deathly cold and rough as granite. Now they were not grey, but almost black or dark green, in places; as though they were covered with lichen. Great stones were embedded in them, and Lynceus even shouted out that high up at mast-head level where he sat in his crow's nest, there was the remains of a man lying, enclosed in this ice and wearing a gold belt about his jerkin.

'Such a man as I have never seen,' he explained. 'He has no beard, no nose to speak of, and only slits in the flesh for eyes.'

To tell truth, I feared that we would never get between the Clashers, for our speed had died off almost completely now. It seemed that we must be crushed, for we had two ship's lengths to go before the clear sea opened out before us again. That being so, I was about to suggest we all abandoned *Argo* and scramble up the sheer ice-faces to look at this man, and perhaps to dig him out and take his gold belt. If we were to die, then what matter if we had a bit of sport first?

But just then Ancaeus took over and yelled out, 'Let each man push on the ice-walls with his oars!'

As they began to do this feverishly, I gave up my notion of leaving the ship and, instead, more to busy my mind than anything else, let loose a white dove from the basket, as an offering to the Mother.

I don't know whether the trick worked or not—you can never prove these things, the prayers of word or deed—but certainly *Argo* seemed to bound along and we were almost out of that grim and silent tunnel when the two floes ground together once more. Tiphys, who had taken over the steering after Ancaeus gave the orders to use the oars, yelled out that

19

the rudder would be crushed, and certainly there was some rending of timber. But we stayed afloat, curvetting like a young horse, and so came clear of the ice.

Atalanta was stretched out on the after-deck, her face to the planks, weeping and beating her hands on the wood. She was like a little child, so terrified that she could hardly speak. I went back to her and shook her by the shoulder.

'There, girl,' I said, 'be brave! Even Hylas didn't make a scene like this when they put him in the water, did he?'

She looked up at me, her eyes bleared and swollen with crying. Then she smiled and it was impossible to believe that she was a priestess; she was no more than a frightened young woman who feared to be hurt, to have her lovely body crushed and cast into the blackness of the deep and silent waters.

I gave her a smack on the backside to cheer her up and then went down among the men. It was bitterly cold but they were all sweating, tearing off their skin hoods and wiping their brows and chests.

Admetus grinned and said, 'Never again, Jason! They can keep their gold in Colchis for all I care! I am for a soft bed before the fire from now on, and anyone can voyage in these seas who cares!'

We all laughed, and I broached a new cask of barley-beer to celebrate. Some of us mulled it over the braziers and we made merry until dusk. It was not every day that one tricked the Clashers.

Death at the Crossroads

Apollo once prophesied to Laius, King of Thebes, that his son, if he had one, would murder his father and then marry his mother. When Laius and his wife, Jocasta, had a son they tried to prevent this prophecy coming true by driving a spike through the boy's feet and leaving him on a mountain-side to die.

In ancient Greece 'exposing' a child like this was a common way for parents to get rid of babies they did not want to keep. Occasionally the baby was found and rescued. Laius's son was found by a shepherd from Corinth who took him to his cottage and adopted him, giving him the name Oedipus, 'swollen-footed', because of the injuries to his feet. Soon afterwards the shepherd took Oedipus to Corinth where King Polybus saw him and decided to adopt him as his own son.

Oedipus grew up quite happily at Corinth, though he was always troubled by the lameness in his feet. Then one day someone at the court accused him of not really being Polybus's son. Oedipus was angry but uncertain. To make sure he went to Delphi to consult the priest of Apollo. The priest told him the dreadful prophecy about murdering his father. In terror Oedipus immediately decided he must leave his happy home at Corinth and go elsewhere. But Thebes was where he decided to go to avoid the danger to his father and mother. Here Oedipus describes how on his journey he met a man he did not know – Laius, King of Thebes – and what happened when they met.

Death at the Crossroads

The road away from Delphi was not an easy one. It lay between mountains and alongside gorges, whose steep pine-clad sides made me afraid, especially by night when, as the path swung to left or right without warning, and my eyes, never keen once the sun had gone down, often did not bring me word of the turning until my crippled feet were at the very lip of the drop. Then, sensing only emptiness and death before me at the next pace, I would stop violently, shivering like a terror-struck horse, pulling back on the rein before an unsuspected obstacle: a dead man or a wall.

So, that is why, on the narrow road between Delphi and Daulis, I was terrified to look down into the deep, stone-strewn gullies below me. And at night when I slept with my cloak round my head on the mountain, I would always drive my javelin as deep as it would go into the earth, and then tether myself to it with thongs from my breeches, so that if I rolled about in my sleeping and my dreaming, this would keep me from going over the edge.

It was a lonely road at this time of the year and I saw no living creatures except eagles, circling the sky above me, and

23

sometimes a red fox trailing his brush as he ran away up the hill slope, trying to pretend that he was not afraid of me, but was suddenly called out on an urgent errand that demanded his attention.

Below Parnassus there is a place where three roads meet, and where, I had always heard, robbers sometimes lurked, to pluck the pigeons on their way to or from the Shrine at Delphi.

At this place I wrapped my cloak tightly round my left arm, to act as some sort of shield should the need for such arise, and my javelin I grasped half-way down its ash-shaft, where I could manage it best for thrusting against swords, daggers or other javelins.

But no one sprang out of the black rocks at me, and I took the middle road that led in the direction of Orchomenus, thinking that it might be broader and less dangerous than the other two. In this I was wrong, for after a while I found that the road shrank to the width of a mere path, with a sheer rock wall on the left, and an unguarded precipice on the right.

It was while I was stumbling along this path, at its narrowest, that, topping a rise which lay before me, a chariot appeared, drawn by two horses and completely filling the roadway. One of its bronze hubs often scraped against the wall of rock, while the bronze tyre of the other wheel ran within a hand's breadth of the precipice. The charioteer who drove it looked very worried as he pulled on the long reins, curbing and guiding his two white and snorting horses. He was a splendid charioteer, though full of fear, and the morning sunlight glistened on his high conical bronze helmet, and on the gold bracers at his wrists. The man who stood at his right hand was much shorter in stature and seemed older, though this was hard to tell because his head was largely covered by a black hood and only the fringe of his grizzled beard jutted out. Yet I could tell that he too was afraid, for he kept his eyes turned away from the precipice under the left wheel, and his brown hands, which gripped the forward chariot-rails, were as white about the knuckles as sun-dried bones.

All this I saw at one glance, as the chariot appeared above the rise, flinging up clouds of dust from the parched roadway. Then I heard the charioteer almost screaming at me, 'Stand aside for the King, you fool! These horses will shy at your staff and we shall be over the edge. Stand aside!'

Now my shepherd-father had brought me up since my childhood to give way to horsemen and charioteers, and I would gladly have done what this proud man ordered if there had been any space at all to move in. But, where we were, if I had pressed against the rocky wall, the chariot-hubs would have broken my legs; and to stand on the hand's breadth which the wheel left, on the precipice side, would have been a certain death, with my lameness and my terror of such heights.

So, with a dry throat and my heart thudding, I called out, 'I ask your pardon, great ones but as you see I am not firm on my feet, and to do as you ask would kill me.'

The charioteer had slowed down his horses until they were walking, but still they came on towards me. I turned about with the intention of running back up the road a mile, to where the three roads met, and where we could have passed one another without any danger.

But suddenly I heard the two men laughing behind me, and then the charioteer shouted, 'We cannot wait all day, cripple, we are on the way to the Oracle and that will brook no delay. So, stand aside for your betters, club-foot!'

As I ran, hearing the horses snorting and the heavy bronze wheels coming up behind me, I suddenly knew that these men did not value my life at all, that they did not care whether I was crushed or whether I fell to my death, that, indeed, they meant to run me down whatever I did. Then I was filled with a great anger for all my life I had tried to be gentle to others and not to harm them without good reason: and these noble charioteers had no reason to harm me whatever.

I think, also, that as the charioteer spoke, as though I was carrion, rubbish, unworthy of life, I remembered how Teiresias had warned me that I must fare forward and take what I wanted from the world, if I was to become a hero. This thought boiled up in my head, as I shambled on before the slavering horses: and, suddenly, the feeling that if I did not make a stand now, I should truly become what the charioteers had said—unworthy rubbish, hardly a man at all.

So, I stopped and, turning, called out, 'I admit no betters save the gods and my father. If you drive at me further I will strike your horses on the nose with this javelin and you will see then, who will step aside.'

As I was speaking, thinking what a great show I was making, I heard the man in the black hood say, with the greatest contempt, 'Wait no longer, Polyphontes, drive over the fool. He is worthless.'

Now indeed, was I in a mortal sweat of terror. Though I grasped my javelin and pointed it towards the horses they loomed up at me as though I had threatened them with a reed, or a cornstalk. I saw their hooves beating down like war-hammers, and I knew that even if I flung myself, I should not escape their crushing blows. I think I wept then, at being crippled and despised by men and women, and even horses. And I think I heard the two charioteers laughing at me as they came on, seeing my tears and my lameness and my despair.

In a less dreadful moment, I am sure that I would have fallen before the horses, begging for pity even: but, suddenly, that cruel laughter from the chariot made me a man, made me all at once careless of the life I had tried to protect. In a moment of extreme clearness, as the horses' heads came closer, spattering me with white froth, I sprang sideways towards the the edge of the precipice. And, as I sprang, I even had the wit to thrust my short javelin into my hide belt, as though it was worth the keeping, however desperate the danger I now faced.

This is a strange thing about men: even in the moment of their greatest peril, there is one small corner of their hearts which rests, in tranquillity, elsewhere; unaffected by the deadly instant. Years later, I saw a Spartan, in the forefront of a spear-charge with barbed arrows flying so thickly at his body that he stood no chance of coming alive out of the charge. And the moment before he fell to his knees, the shafts sticking from him like the quills of a porcupine, he called out to a friend in the next rank, 'Hey, Crotus, did you remember to put the wine in the shade?'

I saw every detail of the chariot, as it drove at me: the chiselled ram's head at the end of the tilt-pole, the careful hide-lashing of each joint in the frame, even the sweat-marks on the forward rail where hands had held it from year to year, marking the polished wood.

Then, as I swung across its path, I saw all the countryside which lay below me, at the foot of the sheer precipice. Beyond the mosses that clung to the cliff-face lay a steeply-sloping pinewood, and against its dark foliage I saw a young eagle, speckled gold against green, darting after a dove. The feathers round that dove's neck were not grey, but of a faintly bluish tinge, and it was chittering with terror, as the eagle came on, its red claws already set forward for the strike, its hooked beak open and its tongue just showing, as though at any moment it would give a shriek of triumph. And far below that, beside a small stream and with five old brown-fleeced sheep about him, grazing, I saw a boy gazing upwards at the eagle, or at me, I do not know which, but with his brown hand shielding

27

his eyes from the morning sun; just as years ago, I had once stood below the rock with my father, waiting for a ruined cattle-breeder to jump down and put an end to all his troubles.

Then I was over the edge, with nothing but the blue air beneath my right foot and my body, and my left foot almost under the whirling chariot wheel. I felt the harsh agony of the bronze as I fell downwards and sideways: but there was no time to cry out. My breath was all needed to let me grasp at the yellow spokes of the wheel. One hand caught and then, by a miracle, the other. My arms were almost torn from my body. My belly and thighs were cruelly rubbed against the rough limestone of the cliff-face. My mouth and eyes were full of dust and grit from the road above me. I heard the charioteer, Polyphontes, cry out, 'Keep still, you brutes. You will have us all over!' I heard his lash striking hard on the backs on the horses.

Then, the swinging of the wheel brought me up and over, with my right foot back on the road, just behind the chariot-deck. And before I lost my balance again and hurtled down into the place from which I had escaped, I cast myself sideways, like a wrestler, and lay choking with relief on the road.

'God,' I cried, 'God, I will repay you. Oh thank you, Lord of Light.'

Then a demon filled my head and as the chariot horses reared and bucked in terror at my wrenching of the wheel and their master's thrashing, I knelt and cast my javelin at Polyphontes' broad back.

It flew, straight as the eagle, and entered between two bronze plates, between his shoulder-blades. I saw him throw up his hands, dropping the reins, to reach backwards at what had hurt him. Then, he gave a shrill squeal, like a woman, or a pig, and leaped sideways, over the low framework of the chariot. And a second later I heard his body crashing down among the pine boughs.

Still on my knees now weaponless, I looked at the chariot. The horses were quiet now, and shuddering with fear. The man in the black hood had turned round and, for the first time, I saw his face. He was that same king who had killed my mother, with one careless blow of his spear butt, eight years ago in Thebes.

Even so, I do not think I should have harmed him for this. I do not think that my wish for vengeance was as strong as my thankfulness at having escaped the chariot and the chasm: and what anger I had felt had largely flowed out of me at seeing Polyphontes the charioteer fall among the pines, where I had been so terrified of falling. No, I would have let this man, this king in his mourning robes, have driven on to wherever he might be bound, I might have flung a stone, or a curse after him, not wishing to strike him or damn him, but only to give vent to my pride in having overcome his action against me.

But his fates, his Furies, would not let him go from that place so easily, would not let me pass on my way without further guilt. And, all at once, he sprang from the still chariot, towards where I kneeled in the dust, with a short bronze sword in his right hand.

This caused no more fear in me, no greater beating of my heart. I waited for him, almost with contempt, and as he slashed down at my head, moved from his slow, old threatening, and caught his arm in my strong hands. I felt his bones, his worn old muscles, his thinness: and for a while I even looked at the brown and wrinkled skin on the back of his hands, with the thick blue veins knotting over them. Then I looked up, smiling, into his watery eyes. He was so old, so harmless, now, that I bore him no grudge. His age was enough punishment I thought, in my young pride. I thought: I am a cripple and a peasant, yet I am greater than a king and his charioteer, greater than two white horses and their war-cart.

I think I would just have shaken him a little, and then have let him go on along the road; but suddenly he brought up his old sharp knee into my face, laughing at my tears and the blood which spurted from my nose. In quick, youthful anger, but still with no true malice, I rose and forced the king back to his war-cart, bending his dry body over the deck to make him humble. Then, for want of something more to punish him, I saw the long, trailing reins of ox-hide, and I looped them round his neck, in contempt.

He stared up at me with a furious terror in his faded eyes. Then he shouted out. 'You gelding! You ruined ox! You thing, you!'

I held him down, laughing, but the two horses, made sensitive by their ordeal on the narrow path, took fright at his shrill and sudden voice and whisked their cart away, and the bound king with it. He flew from my hands, backwards, tangled in the reins and screaming. The dust rose round him as he twirled along the road, like a great fish being drawn from the sea, and fighting with old, veined hands all the while, to keep the reins from throttling him.

Had his luck held, with all his struggling he should have torn himself free within a few yards: but, suddenly, as though they had come to the end of their struggling, their war with the world, the white horses plunged sideways, towards the precipice. One wheel of their chariot broke down the lip of rock that kept them safe, then the whole cart lurched, scattering chips of limestone, and the great pole with its bronze ram's head heeled over.

Amid the grey dust, and under the hot blue sky, first one white horse, then the other slewed sideways and fell, galloping still in the empty air, with mane and tail soaring upwards and as stiff as carved stone: then went the chariot, cracking and crumbling, flinging its pieces back onto the path where I stood, the bronze sword hanging in my hand still. And last of all went the black-robed king still clutching at the reins about his throat, still staring wide-eyed up at the blue sky as though the god might yet come down and wrench him away from the falling; but still screaming out, in his old man's hoarse voice.

As he slid over the edge and out of my sight, I started to run forward, as though, even now, I might save him.

But all at once a brown snake slithered through the white dust, at my feet, from a parched bush of lavender, and coiled, hissing, before me, its flat head darting here and there sideways, halting me.

I stopped, struck at it with the king's sword, and missed the mark. Then I heard that sickening crashing among the pine-trees and forgot the snake for a moment.

When I remembered it again, it had gone, leaving only its crooked trail across the white dust of the mountain road.

The Return of Agamemnon

For ten years King Agamemnon was away from home commanding the Greek forces at the siege of Troy. When Troy fell Agamemnon took as his mistress a beautiful captive, Cassandra, the daughter of the slaughtered king of Troy. Agamemnon's wife Clytemnestra was bitterly angry with her husband because at the beginning of the expedition he had ordered the sacrifice of their daughter Iphigenia to placate a goddess whom he had offended. Resentment at this had driven Clytemnestra to take her husband's cousin Aegisthus as her lover. When Agamemnon returned from Troy with Cassandra, Clytemnestra arranged to murder them both.

There were varying accounts of the death of Agamemnon. Homer preferred the guilty love of a man and a woman as the motive, and in the Odyssey the spirit of Agamemnon tells how he and his men were set upon and killed by Clytemnestra and Aegisthus as they feasted after their return. Aeschylus, writing much later, had as the motive a wife's determination to avenge the death of a daughter she had loved. It is the version of Aeschylus that has been adopted by Henry Treece, and Agamemnon's other daughter, Electra, whose aid has been enlisted by her mother, here tells of her father's return and murder.

The Return of Agamemnon

It had been ten years since I last saw my father, and I do not know now what I expected to see that day—a rich prince? A god? Or a man raised from the dead?

I think it must have been the last, for, as in a dream, I saw this man standing on a broken cart and knew him at once, though he was like no king that the world had ever seen before. The hair had gone from his brown and wrinkled head; his beard, that had once been his lion's pride, was but a few thin hairs that blew about in the wind on our upland rocks; his nose had shrunk until it looked a bird's beak, above which his filmed grey eyes gazed, like those of a timeless mariner who must search for some lost coast-line to eternity, blinding himself.

I saw his shoulder-bones almost poking up through his salt-caked hide; the grizzled mat of grey hairs that shrouded his body from throat to waist; the palsied twitching of his great hands on the reins—and I thought: Is this the man I hate? Is this the man who has brought fear and agony to Hellas, to my family?

As the late sun struck down between two pillars on to him,

I saw Agamemnon clearly for the first time in my life. He was nothing but a blind old man, a dreamer who has lost his dream, a warrior no longer strong enough to shake a sword. This was the High King of Achaea.

And I looked at my mother, and she was an old woman; no longer beautiful, noble only in name, a gasping creature leaning on a grey stone wall and trying to remember the fire, the rage of youth.

Put the two of them together, out on the road to Delphi, and any peasant would throw an offering of bread to them; no farmer with two acres to his name would stand aside to let them pass. . . .

Then all at once I heard my mother call, 'There she is, the Trojan's daughter. There is his woman and her children!'

Sitting behind Agamemnon in the cart was a girl about my own age, a soiled grey cloth over her black hair, like a headdress, and a torn robe of wool bound roughly round her body with hide thongs. At her thin breast she suckled one baby; at her side stood a pale, grey-eyed boy, his slack mouth open and the moisture dribbling from it on to his torn shirt.

Aegisthus had time to sneer and say, 'So, this is Cassandra, who foretells the future—if only she could get anyone to listen to her! In truth, King Priam must have been a crofter-king, some jumped-up peasant, to father such kin!'

Then King Agamemnon came within hearing distance, and all the folk looked to us to give him the proper greeting. I glanced at my brother in his armour, and saw the tears welling in his eyes that this old scarecrow should be his father. Hermione put her arms about him and tried to console him, but he shook her away rudely.

Then Clytemnestra went forward with difficulty, leaning on her handmaids, and stopped in front of the two oxen that dragged the High King's cart.

Somehow she found strength to call in a high, clear voice, 'Greetings, Lion of Hellas; We of your House come out to meet you. How went the war in Troy, my lord?'

Agamemnon bent his head, as though it was painful for him to move his neck, and stared like a man trying to see through a heavy mist. His blank grey eyes wavered for a while, then seemed to find my mother. He held out his hands widely, in the ritual gesture, and said, 'Some died on either side, my wife. But in the end the god gave us the victory and the honour. We return with tribute and in peace.'

Neither of them made reference to Cassandra or to Aegisthus; but Clytemnestra took the head-band of the ox nearest to her and made the motion of leading the cart up towards the palace. As she went, each step a penance, her handmaids close behind her lest she fell, Orestes and I walked at the tail of the cart in silence. Our father half-turned and saw us, his mouth twitching and his brows moving up and down, like a very old man who is beating his brains to remember, but cannot.

I saw that he had forgotten who we were, and this gave me no pain at all. I only wished that Agamemnon had died in the outland, under the Trojan walls—then we could have hated him as much as we chose, but we should have been forced to remember him with respect. Now, he was nothing, a man more valued in death than in this poor life he dragged about on his bent back.

As we went, a great hush fell on the crowd; then, when we were some distance away, a deep, rumbling laughter rose, as though all the poor folk now saw that they were the great ones, not Agamemnon, that they were free at last, and he a broken prisoner to a dream.

Then, up the hill came the Thebans, with the Ithacan contingent who had lost their king and were singing the most lewd and disrespectful ballads about him. The crowd turned away from us, and I was glad.

When we reached the palace steps, Clytemnestra held out her hand to help Agamemnon down, as was her wifely duty; but he had great trouble in making his legs do what he wished, and in the end he almost tumbled from the cart into the dust. The line of Cretan guards upon the steps began to smile at this, at first behind their hands, then quite openly. But my father did not seem to hear them. He turned towards Cassandra and said, 'There is that to do, inside, my dear. Soon they will bid you to the feast. They will treat you well, have no fear.'

As he spoke, the girl buried her face in her hands and began to moan, the baby at her breast forgotten. The boy beside her in the cart moved forward and took the child gently in his own thin hands.

I was standing beside my mother when this happened. Her face was like an ivory mask of tragedy, so wide were her eyes, so twisted down the corners of her gaping mouth. It was as though she tried to weep, but no tears would come.

She whispered to me, as Agamemnon mounted the long flight of steps, 'Oh god, Electra, I cannot do it now that the time has come. He has paid already, daughter. I cannot do it, I tell you. It rests with you now!'

Then Agamemnon stopped, his hand over his heart, breathing heavily and waving his head about, seeking my mother. 'Where is the Amber Princess?' he asked, in his dry old voice. 'Where is my little girl-thing then? I thought she would be the first to greet me when I came back to my house.'

I wanted to turn and race down the long stairway. I was ashamed of myself, of him, of the very world itself. But I dared not run away, and I dared not go to him now.

Clytemnestra stood beside him and said, 'She is resting,

Great One. She will soon come to see you, to show you her new corn doll.'

She spoke to him as though he was a simpleton, and he nodded and smiled towards her. 'I thank you, lady,' he said. 'These little girls must have their rest, and their dolls, if they are to grow up in healthy contentment. A child of eleven needs her rest. Sleep puts roses in the cheeks and starlight in the eyes. One day, my Amber girl shall marry a great . . .'

He broke off then and sat down on a carved stone lion that stood against the balustrade, sighing and trying to get his breath.

'I had a son. Oh, years ago. He must be dead and in the tomb now. Orestes, they called him. By the god, but time flies! I can only picture him as a baby. . . . A baby, tottering from stool to stool, with the milk round his mouth. It is all most strange. Surely, he was a great warrior?'

He pursed his lips and then began to cough. A small patch of red showed suddenly on his cheekbones and a vein throbbed under the parchment skin of his forehead.

He ran his knotted fingers over the carved name of the stone lion and said all at once, 'On one of the islands we called at—I forget—Cassandra would tell you—close by Leros, I think, or just south of Delos—one of those places—'

His voice faded away, and he began to look round to find the stone lion's tail. Clytemnestra stood over him and said gently, 'What was this you saw, on the island, High King?'

Agamemnon looked up at her with a blank face, as though he had never seen her in his life before. He answered slowly, 'Why, a tortoise, lady. Bigger than a bull, and older than Zeus, they said on the island. I saw three men sit on his shell and go riding. The sound of his eating at midday was like lightning crackling. No, not lightning. Like a herd of wild cows rushing through brushwood. No, not like that either. Like . . .'

He got up and said, 'Why do you keep me with such foolish talk, woman? Where is the bath-house in this place? Hey, where is the bath-house? I am weary from my journey. Lead me there, I command you.'

The queen, my mother, nodded to old Geilissa to take Agamemnon where he had said. He went with her quietly, not raising his voice again. And, as they entered into the great hall, my mother turned to me and said, 'Well, Electra, now there is no other way. You heard him ask for the bath-house? That is as the omens have foretold—he has asked his way to his death-place. What can we do now but let his pattern run on to the end?'

She spoke so quietly, almost with tenderness, that there, in the sun on the high steps of the palace, I could see no other way, though I tried my hardest to find one, I swear.

I said, 'But I cannot do it, mother. Now that he asks for it, I cannot do it. Yesterday, last month, any other time, and I would have gloried in it—but now all that has gone.'

She leaned against the stone lion and nodded. 'I am the same, my love,' she whispered. 'Yet it must be done. You see he is the husk of a man, he is as good as dead already. To-morrow, or the next day, another will put an end to him—or worse, will drag him off as a hostage to some place where we shall never find him. Better to put him out of his misery now; then we shall know his end.'

I said, 'Very well; what am I to do?' There was nothing else to say:

Clytemnestra answered in a still, dead voice, 'Go into the bath-house when he is ready and wrap the towel round him, as though you are a servant-girl sent to dry him. But, I beg you, see that the cloth goes round his arms, not under them.

This must be done quickly, with no fuss. I do not think I could carry out the task if he broke away and tried to save himself. Take one of the strong new towels, not the old threadbare ones.'

I shook the tears from my eyes. 'I will do as you say, mother,' I told her.

Steam made the air heavy, and the serving-women moved through it like ghosts, pouring in water and more water from wooden buckets. When I sent them away, they bowed and did not speak. They saw the thick towel in my hands and knew what I had come for. That towel was of the sacred fleece, the Kin-sign of all the House of Atreus.

It was a while before I saw him, lolling in the deep bath, swishing the water between his thighs like a little boy. He could not see me bending over him for the steam, or for his half-blind eyes, I know not which.

I said softly, 'Rise, High King. I have come to put the cloth about you.'

Agamemnon stared down at the water and said, 'I am not such a fool that I do not know why you have come, Electra.'

Then, as I stood, shocked, he smiled at me and whispered. 'I shall give you no trouble, my dear. I know the rite; I rise, I place one foot on dry land, one in water, and so I stand until the axe falls. Is it still the axe in Mycenae, Electra? So many other things seem to have changed.'

I nodded down at him and said, 'It is still the axe, sir.'

He splashed the water with his hands a little while, then he said, 'You have not mentioned Iphigenia, my dear. I thought you would speak of her at this time.'

When he said this, so simply, I knew that I wished him dead again, although I had felt such pity for him on the palace steps in the sunlight.

I said shortly, 'Rise, sir, I am waiting.'

41

My heart was smacking at my ribs. I was listening for Clytemnestra to come along the passage-way so that all might be done according to the custom. Agamemnon was listening, too. As he rose, with some difficulty, he said, 'She is keeping us waiting, Amber! It was always her way. But she does not look so well, does she, daughter? Is she sick?'

I was angry and afraid, the thick mist of steam in the bath-house half-choked me. My shift was sodden and clung to me, chilling my body, though my face burned as if I stood before a furnace.

I almost shouted, 'Will you come out, or must I fetch you, sir?'

Agamemnon looked at me with wrinkled eyelids, and even smiled. 'It is strange,' he said, as though to himself, 'but I have stood where arrows hailed and spears thudded, where horses reared and swords crashed down, for ten long years—yet I do not recall ever being so afraid as I am now, my daughter. Perhaps it is true what Achilles once said, that I have the face of a hound, but the heart of a deer!'

It was as he was saying this, and clambering out from the deep bath, that dark shapes moved in the steam. I heard Agamemnon give a little intake of the breath, as though he was about to sneeze, then, as I wrapped the woollen cloth about him, I saw it grow suddenly bright with blood. He slipped a little way into my arms, so that I had to support his weight, sitting on the lip of the bath.

Yet it was small weight enough; he was as light as a child, for all his great frame and the grizzled pelt of his body.

He coughed twice, then turned his head up sideways and fixed me with his flinty grey eye. 'It was not my doing—Iphigenia,' he said. 'It was the priest Calchas, and goatherd Aegisthus. They shed her blood.'

As he spoke, the red kept coming from him, down on to my

42

lap and over my breast, in great spurts. Now there were two dark shapes in the steamy chamber. I could scarcely breathe for the water and the blood. I was glad, at last, when I saw my mother come out of the mist and strike down twice with the stone axe we kept above the Hearth Shrine.

The Fight for Freedom

Ivan Yefremov's book, *Land of Foam*, is about the travels of a young Greek sculptor, Pandion, in foreign lands – especially in Egypt, where he becomes a slave and makes a dramatic escape. Yefremov describes in vivid and startling detail what he thinks an Egyptian slave's life was like.

This chapter tells of the slaves plotting their escape. Yefremov seems to be particularly struck by the contrast between the low value set on a slave's life and the fact that the slaves were often, as he portrays them, people of originality and character.

It is not quite clear when the events in this book take place, since at one point Pandion watches a bull-leaping display in Crete, and yet sculptures are described which belong to a much later date (mid-fifth century B.C.).

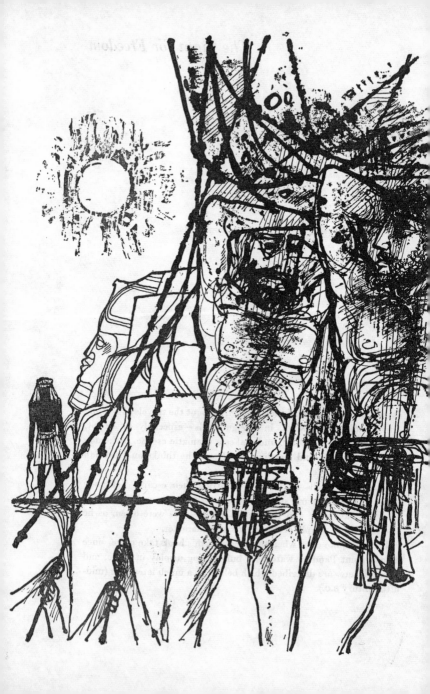

The Fight for Freedom

The stones, heated by the blazing sun, burned the arms and shoulders of the slaves. The gentle breeze brought no coolness to them, but instead aggravated their plight by covering them with fine dust from the stones which ate into their eyes.

Thirty slaves, already at the end of their strength, were pulling on stiff ropes to raise onto the wall a heavy stone slab bearing a bas-relief of some sort. The slab had to be placed in a prepared nest at a height of some eight cubits from the ground. Four experienced and nimble slaves were steadying the slab from below. Among them was Pandion who stood next to an Egyptian, the only inhabitant of Aigyptos among the many nations in their slave compound. This Egyptian, condemned to eternal slavery for some unknown, awful crime he had committed, occupied the end cell in the privileged southeastern corner of the shehne.[1] Two purple brands in the shape of a wide cross covered his chest and back while on his cheek a red snake was branded. Morose, never smiling, he did not talk to anybody and, despite the horror of his own position, despised the foreign slaves in the same way that his free fellow countrymen did.

[1] *shehne:* barrack block in a prison camp.

At the present moment he was not paying any attention to anybody and, with his shaven head lowered, was pressing with his hands against the heavy stone to prevent it from swaying.

Suddenly Pandion noticed that the strands of a rope holding the stone were beginning to snap, and shouted to warn the others. Two of the slaves jumped to one side but the Egyptian paid no attention to Pandion and could not see what was going on above his head—he remained standing under the heavy stone.

With a wide sweep of his right arm, Pandion gave the Egyptian a shove in the chest that sent him flying clear of the danger spot. At that very moment the rope snapped and the stone crashed down, grazing Pandion's hand as it fell. A yellowish pallor spread over the Egyptian's face. The stone struck against the foot of the wall and a big piece was broken off the corner of the bas-relief.

The overseer came running toward Pandion with a shout of rage and lashed at him with his whip. The square hippopotamus-hide lash, two fingers thick, cut deeply into the small of Pandion's back. The pain was so great that everything went misty before his eyes.

'You wastrel, why did you save that carrion?' howled the overseer, slashing at Pandion a second time. 'The stone would have remained whole if it had fallen on a soft body. That carving is worth more than the lives of hundreds of creatures like you,' he added as the second blow struck home.

Pandion would have rushed at the overseer but he was seized by the soldiers, who hurried to the scene and brutally thrashed him.

That night Pandion lay face downward in his cell. He was in a high fever, the deep whip cuts on his back, shoulders and legs were inflamed. Kidogo came crawling to him and brought him water to drink, from time to time pouring water over his aching head.

A slight rustling sound came from outside the door, followed by a whisper: 'Ekwesha, are you there?'

Pandion answered and felt somebody's hands laid on him in the darkness.

It was the Egyptian. He took a tiny jar out of his belt and spent a long time rubbing something into the palms of his hands. Then he began to pass his hands carefully over Pandion's weals, spreading some liquid unguent with an acrid, unpleasant smell. The pain made the Hellene shudder but the confident hands of the Egyptian continued their work. By the time the Egyptian began to massage the legs, the pain in Pandion's back had died away; a few minutes later Pandion dropped quietly off to sleep.

'What did you do to him?' whispered Kidogo who was quite invisible in his corner.

After a short pause the Egyptian answered him: 'This is *kiphi*, it's the finest ointment, and the secret is known only to our priesthood. My mother brought it here by paying a big bribe to a soldier.'

From that day onward the Egyptian made friends with the young Hellene although he still ignored his companions. After that Pandion often heard a rustling sound near his cell and if he was alone the lean, bony body of the Egyptian would come crawling in. The lonely, embittered son of Tha-Quem was outspoken and talkative when he was alone with the sympathetic Pandion, who soon learned the Egyptian's story.

Yakhmos, the son of the moon, came from an old family of *nedshes*, faithful servants of former Pharaohs who had lost their position and their wealth with a change of dynasty. Yakhmos had had a good schooling and had been employed as scribe by the Governor of the Province of the Hare. He chanced to fall in love with the daughter of a builder who demanded that his son-in-law be a man of means. Yakhmos lost his head for love of the girl, and turned to robbery of the royal tombs as a means to speedy enrichment. Soon he had large quantities of gold in his hands but in the meantime the girl had been given in marriage to an official in the far south.

Yakhmos tried to drown his sorrows in merry feasting and the purchase of concubines, and the money soon melted away. The dark road to wealth was already known to him and he again set out to do nefarious deeds. He told of his adventures in the fearful underground labyrinths, where death awaited the intruder at every step from traps cunningly designed by the builders.

In the oldest tombs that lay deep below the huge pyramids the treasures and the royal sarcophagi were protected by huge, thick slabs of stone that closed the gangways. The later tombs were in a labyrinth of false corridors that ended in deep wells with smooth walls. Huge blocks of stone fell from above when the intruders tried to move the stones that protected the tombs, heaps of sand shot down through wells from above and barred their way forward. If the bold intruders tried to pass the sand and penetrated deeper into the tombs, more earth showered down on them from the wells and buried the robbers in a narrow passage between the sand heaps and the newly fallen earth. In the newer tombs stone jaws closed noiselessly in the darkness of the narrow tunnels or a frame studded with sharp spears crashed down from the columns immediately the intruder set his foot on a certain fatal stone in the floor.

Yakhmos and his companions had spent many nights on the verge of the Western Desert where the Cities of the Dead stretched for thousands of cubits. Hiding in the darkness, not daring to speak or strike a light, feeling their way to the howl of the jackals, the laughing of the hyenas and the menacing roar of the lions, the plunderers dug their way through stifling passages or cut through whole cliffs in an effort to find the direction in which the deeply hidden tomb lay.

Pandion listened in amazement and horror to the tales of adventure told by this thin, insignificant man who had so often risked his life for the sake of a few moments' pleasure, and could not understand him.

'Why did you continue living like that?' Pandion asked him one night. 'Why couldn't you go away?'

The Egyptian smiled a silent, mirthless smile.

'The Land of Quemt is a strange land. You, a foreigner, cannot understand her. We are all imprisoned here. In the west is the desert—the kingdom of death. The desert in the east is passable only to large caravans with a good supply of water. In the south there are savage tribes hostile to us. All our neighbours burn with hatred against our country whose well-being is founded on the misfortunes of weaker peoples.

'You're not a son of Tha-Quem and can't understand how we fear to die in a strange land. In this valley of the Hapi, everywhere alike, where our ancestors have lived for thousands of years and tilled the soil, dug canals and made fertile the land, we, too, must live and die. Tha-Quem is shut off from the world and that lies like a curse upon us. When there are too many people their lives are of no value—and there is nowhere for us to migrate to, the people chosen by the gods are not loved by the peoples of foreign lands ...'

'But would it not be better for you to flee now that you're a slave?' asked Pandion.

'Alone and branded?' came the Egyptian's ejaculation of astonishment. 'I'm now worse than a foreigner ... Remember, Ekwesha, there's no escaping from here!'

At Pandion's request Yakhmos drew a plan of the Land of

51

Quemt in a patch of moonlight on the floor. The young Hellene was horrified: he was in the very middle of the valley of a great river thousands of stadia in length. There was water and life to the north and south but to get there through a densely populated land with countless military fortifications was impossible. In the empty deserts on either side there was no population nor was there any means of subsistence.

The few caravan roads along which there were wells were strongly guarded.

After the Egyptian had left him, Pandion spent a sleepless night trying to think out a plan of escape.

The next night Pandion crawled to the cell of the Etruscan, Cavius, told him all he had learned from the Egyptian and tried to persuade him to make an attempt to arouse the slaves to rebellion. Cavius did not answer him but sat stroking his beard, deep in thought. Pandion was well aware that preparations for rebellion had long been under way and that the various tribal groups had chosen their leaders.

'I can't stand it any longer, why should we wait?' exclaimed Pandion passionately; Cavius hurriedly put his hand over his mouth. 'Better death,' added the Hellene, somewhat more calmly. 'What is there to wait for? Are you afraid of death or what?'

Cavius raised his hand.

'I'm not afraid and you know it,' he said brusquely, 'but we have five hundred lives dependent on us. Do you propose to sacrifice them? You'll get your death at a high price.'

Pandion struck his head against the low ceiling as he sat up suddenly in his impatience.

'I'll think it over and talk to people,' Cavius hastened to add, 'but still it's a pity there are only two other shehne near us and that we have no access to them. We'll talk tomorrow night and I'll let you know. Tell Kidogo to come . . .'

Pandion left Cavius' cell, crawled hurriedly along the wall so as to get there before the moon rose, and made for Yakhmos' cell. Yakhmos was still awake.

'I went to see you,' whispered the Egyptian in excited tones, 'but you weren't there. I wanted to tell . . .' he stammered. 'I've been told that I'm being taken away from here tomorrow; they are sending three hundred men to the gold mines in the desert. That's how matters stand—nobody ever comes back from there . . .'

'Why?' asked Pandion.

'Slaves sent to work there rarely live more than a year. There's nothing worse than the work down there amid the sun-baked rocks, with no air to breathe. They give them very little water as there isn't enough to go round. The work consists of breaking hard stones and carrying the ore in baskets. The strongest of the slaves drop exhausted at the end of the day's work and blood runs from their ears and throats . . . Farewell, Ekwesha, you're a fine fellow although you did me a bad turn by saving my life. It's not the rescue that I value but the sympathy you showed me . . .'

Overcome by pity, the young Hellene drew nearer to the Egyptian.

'But you can take your own . . .' Pandion stopped short.

Yakhmos staggered back from him.

'What are you saying, foreigner? Do you imagine I can allow my *Ka*[1] to torment my *Ba*[2] for all eternity in never ending sufferings? . . .'

Pandion understood nothing of what the Egyptian was saying. He sincerely believed that suffering ends with death but did not say so out of tolerance for the faith of the Egyptian.

[1] *Ka:* the soul of the intellect.
[2] *Ba:* the corporal soul, the spirit of the body.

Yakhmos pushed aside the straw on which he slept at night and began digging in the corner of his cell.

'Here, take this dagger, if ever you dare ... and this will remind you of me if a miracle happens and you gain your liberty.' Yakhmos placed a smooth, cold object in Pandion's hand.

'What's that? What do I want it for?'

'It's a stone I found in the underground rooms of an old temple hidden among the rocks.'

The colouring of the stone reminded Pandion of something that was very familiar to him. Its reflection brought warmth to the youth's heavy heart. *Thalassa!* The sea. It was exactly that colour, far from the shore, at the time when the sun hung high in the blue heavens. *Natur a'e*, the divine stone, is what the unfortunate Yakhmos had called it!

The menacing roll of the big drum thundered over the cells—this was the signal arousing the slaves for their day's work.

Pandion made a momentary decision and secreted the unusual stone in his loincloth. He would not leave that symbol of the free sea in the dusty earth of the shehne. Let it remain with him always.

On the journey and during their work in the gardens Pandion watched Cavius carefully and noticed that the latter was constantly exchanging short phrases first with one and then with another of the shehne leaders known to Pandion. These immediately went away from the Etruscan and talked to their followers.

Pandion chose a safe moment and drew near Cavius. The Etruscan did not raise his head from the stone he was dressing but spoke softly and quickly, without even taking breath.

'Tonight, before the moon rises, in the end gallery of the northern wall ...'

Pandion returned to his work. On the way back to the shehne he passed Cavius' message on to Kidogo.

As soon as the compound had quieted down and the sentries on the wall were dozing, Kidogo appeared in the darkness of Pandion's cell.

The two friends crawled quickly to the wall and turned into the narrow corridor between the cells. They reached the north wall where the shadows in the corridor were deepest of all. The sentries rarely walked along this wall, they could observe the compound more easily from the western and eastern walls, looking along the corridors between the cells. There was, therefore, no danger that the sentries above would hear their whispered conversation.

No less than sixty slaves lay in two rows in the corridor, their feet pressed against the walls and their heads together. Cavius and Remdus were in the middle. The elder Etruscan called Pandion and Kidogo to him in a whisper.

Feeling for the Etruscan's hand, Pandion passed to him the dagger he had brought with him. Cavius felt the cold metal in some perplexity, cut his hand on the sharp blade and then avidly gripped the weapon, whispering his thanks.

The experienced old soldier had yearned for weapons and the dagger brought joy to his heart. He also realized that by handing the precious dagger over to him the Hellene recognized his seniority and had, without words, elected him the leader.

He did not stop to ask Pandion where he had got the dagger, but began to talk in whispers, making long pauses so that those near him could pass his words on to their more distant comrades who were out of hearing.

Cavius said that the rebellion could not be put off any longer, that there was no hope in the future, the situation would only get worse if the slaves were again broken up into groups and sent in different directions.

55

'The strength that is our only guarantee of success in struggle is being undermined by the heavy drudgery required by our taskmasters; every month in captivity means loss of health and vitality. Death in battle is honourable and joyful; it is a thousand times easier to die in battle than to die under the blows of a whip.'

A unanimous whisper of approval passed along the rows of invisible listeners.

'We must not delay the revolt,' continued Cavius, 'but there is one condition that must be fulfilled: we must find a way out of this accursed country. Even if we are joined by two or three other shehne, even if we are able to get weapons, our forces will still be small and we shall not be able to hold out for long. Ever since the Great Revolt of the slaves the rulers of Quemt have done everything possible to keep the slaves divided in separate compounds, we have no contact with the others and we shall not be able to arouse a large number of people simultaneously. We are right in the capital, where there are many soldiers, and we shall not be able to fight our way through the country. The archers of Aigyptos are a terrible force; we shall not have many bows, and not everybody will be able to use them. Let us think whether we can make our way through the desert to the east or the west. We may find ourselves in the desert shortly after leaving the shehne. If we are unable to cross the desert, then I think we must drop the idea of a revolt—it will be a useless waste of effort and a tormenting death. Then let only those of us flee that are prepared to make the attempt to pass through certain death with a faint hope of liberty. I, for example, will make the attempt.'

The Wrestling School

Leon and Hippias are two boys who went to school in Athens a short time before the first Persian invasion of Greece in 490 B.C. They have each shown unusual ability for their age at athletics and because of this have been granted special permission to attend the Gymnasium for training. But on the day of their first visit they were fooling around stupidly and hit one of the attendants with a discus. Luckily, because the attendant was a slave and was not badly hurt, their punishment was not severe. They were expelled from the Gymnasium for a week and warned that the consequences would be serious if their behaviour was not more sensible in future. In the following passage we learn what kind of day they had at the Gymnasium a week later when they made a fresh start.

The Wrestling School

Leon and Hippias again took care to be at the gymnasium in good time when their week's expulsion had elapsed. This time, however, they were even more careful not to meddle with the gear. Instead, they asked pardon of the unfortunate attendant whom they had wounded, and gave him a generous tip. 'And after all,' Hippias reminded him, 'you were only hurt in one place and it's healed already, but our backs caught it all over, and they're aching yet.'

'That sounds all right, Sir,' the attendant grumbled, 'but your backs will have nothing much to show for it, and I shall carry the scar to my grave. And if ever I'm killed in battle, people will see it and think I got stabbed trying to run away!'

Rather unfeelingly, the boys laughed, but they quickly hushed their mirth when the supervisor sent for them.

'Now, Leon, son of Charmides,' he began in formal tones. 'You understand that this is not a mere palaestra. It's intended for men, not for boys, and it's a great privilege that you're allowed here. We granted it because we had a good report of your promise as an athlete; take care that your conduct doesn't make us feel we've made a mistake. And that, Hippias, applies also to you—do you understand? Let there be no more nonsense such as we had before.'

Sternly as he spoke, a twinkle in his eye suggested that he too was conscious of the humorous aspects of that 'nonsense'. None the less, the boys dared not smile, and were glad to be handed over to the instructors. As Hippias went over for wrestling practice, Leon felt very much the new boy and very much alone.

'Now,' the instructor commanded, 'let's see how you shape.' Leon obediently slipped off his tunic and handed it to a grinning slave-boy. Feeling very self-conscious, he stood there naked while the instructor eyed him up and down and felt his muscle and prodded him as though he were a slave put up for sale. Then he was made to walk up and down, to take a short run, to jump, to 'go through the motions' of casting a javelin and hurling a discus, and to perform other antics, while the instructor looked critically on and the slave-boy seemed to be trying to hide a grin.

At last the instructor gave a sniff which might have meant anything but did not sound at all complimentary, and told Leon to join a squad of beginners. An oldish slave came forward, and stood patiently waiting while the instructor fastened a curious harness round his head and beneath his mouth. As he raised a flute to its lips the purpose of this became apparent; it was to help support the rather clumsy instrument that he played, and to save his cheeks from being strained with too much blowing.

A few words of instruction; then, as the flute emitted its bird-like notes, the squad began one of the 'dances' which formed the backbone of athletic training among the Hellenes—really a musical drill, designed to exercise rhythmically every part of the body. At first, however, it did not proceed without interruption—the instructor, whose method of correction was 'a word and a blow and the blow first', was ready to check the slightest inattention or incorrectness of movement. Leon suffered an occasional taste of his stick, but was relieved to find that he fared better than some of the others.

There was a pause and a well-earned rest, then systematic training began in running. One by one the trainees were called out and made to stand in the correct starting position for a foot-race; 'take your stand foot to foot,' the instructor called it. Two parallel grooves a few inches apart were scored in the gymnasium floor. As his turn came, Leon took his place, the toes of his left foot touching the foremost of the two lines— 'and if they so much as overlap by a hair's breadth,' the instructor warned him, 'you'll feel the weight of my stick.' The toes of his right foot were very slightly in advance of the second line (that didn't matter, the distance between them was suited to a grown man, not a boy) and just touching his left instep. Raising his right arm to keep his balance he bent his knees, leant forward slightly, and stood waiting alertly, ready for the word to start.

He was somewhat perturbed when the instructor raised a forked stick menacingly above him, and wondered if *that* were to give the starting signal. But it did not fall.

The supervisor, looking very impressive with his flowing beard and his long robe, and with a fillet bound round his head, now came forward and stood near him with extended arm. 'Steady on the mark,' he commanded, and Leon fixed his gaze on the end of the course, about 200 yards away; for this was the length of the stadium at Olympia and formed the shortest race of all, the popular stade-race.

'Go!' and Leon bounded away; he knew from his experience in the palaestra and from general talk the need for making a good start. He dashed with all his might down the track, and was gratified to hear a murmur of applause from some of the spectators.

The supervisor said nothing, but the instructor had a few cutting things to say about Leon's style. The boy was relieved at being allowed to stand aside and watch while his comrades showed their paces.

Each of them, like himself, was menaced by the instructor's uplifted rod, and once or twice this fell heavily, producing a yelp of pain. Its purpose was now evident: it was simply to punish anyone who made a false start and got his foot off the line before the word 'Go'. Leon made up his mind that he would take care never to make that mistake.

Further 'dances' followed, and then the trainees paused for lunch, first cooling their heated bodies. Leon intended to stand under one of the ornamental lion's heads, whose mouths spurted streams of water, but Hippias checked him. 'They're only for the men,' he explained, 'we'll just have to pour buckets of water over each other—so.' And Leon spluttered and gasped at his unexpected drenching, and then revenged himself by drenching Hippias; they were just beginning a pleasant little water-fight when one of the attendants checked them with a blow or two of his rod.

Lunch was a cheerful affair, the food the boys had brought being pooled: Leon's bread and cheese, grapes which Hippias had brought and some sausage generously contributed by one of the men. After the meal they sat about gossiping in true Athenian style—except that instead of discussing public affairs they talked about matters more important to themselves, the manners and appearance of the instructors.

During the afternoon dancing was again followed by further running practice. 'We'll try a diaulos this time,' the instructor decided, 'so that you can practise turning.' For this was twice the length of the stade-race, about 400 yards; at its far end the runners had to swing round a post before returning on their tracks, and to do it without losing too much speed. Again the supervisor came to look on while Leon was running, and again he went away without a word.

'Next thing,' said the instructor, while an attendant handed out a number of small handy picks, 'you can loosen up the surface of the *skamma*. It's good for training, too, especially for boxers and wrestlers; loosens up the muscles as well as the sand.'

'If he thinks it's so good, it's a pity he doesn't do it himself,' commented Hippias, but he was careful to speak under his breath. Obediently he and the other boys took the picks and hacked up the sand in the jumping-pit; beaten by the impact of feet and bodies and baked by the sunshine, it had got very hard: to land on it with any force would be to risk a sprained ankle.

Here again there were lines to be 'toe'd' when the jump took place, and as before the instructor menaced with his rod anyone who looked like overstepping the mark. The elderly slave adjusted his face-harness and raised his flute to his lips: for this exercise, too, had to be carried out to music.

A standing long jump had to be made from lines at the edge of the sand-pit. As each of the trainees landed, a line was scored on the sand where his feet had touched, and the instructor measured the distance covered with his rod. Faults in style were indicated, with a touch of the rod to emphasize them.

'Now,' the instructor told them, 'you can do the jump properly, with the halteres.'[1] Grasping a pair of jumping-weights, an advanced student gave a demonstration of their use, while the class watched intently.

---

[1] *halteres*: weights held in the hand and used to help athletes to jump further. They looked rather like dumb-bells.

'Remember this,' the instructor warned them, 'the jump doesn't count unless your footprints are regular. If you land one foot before the other, or if you fall or so much as stumble, then it's a false jump, and we won't even trouble to find out how far you've gone. The important thing isn't to cover the ground, but to show correct style.'

But there were no false jumps in the demonstration. Grasping a weight in either hand, the student nodded to the flute-player. As the musical notes shrilled out, he swung the weights head-high before him; paused, swung them forcibly downwards and bent slightly; paused when his hands were just under his knees, and swung his weights forwards. Again he swung them backwards and then again forwards and then backwards once more. But now, on the forward swing, by vigorously straightening his body and knees, he launched himself into the air. He swung legs and arms forward ready to land; but at the last moment he again swung his arms backwards; and the recoil, as the heavy jumping-weights went behind him, thrust him on, increasing the length of his jump. The class broke into a hum of appreciation as he made a perfect landing, and even the instructor gave him a grudging word of praise.

By contrast the leaps of the class were not merely short but ridiculously clumsy, and the instructor had some acid remarks to make, driving the moral home with blows of his stick. Then he made them practise swinging their arms while grasping the jumping weights tightly. The music of the flute turned the exercise into a dance.

The class now returned to the actual jumping, with the halteres to assist them. Then a feeling seemed to spread that it was time for the day's work to cease. When a slave had collected the weights and taken them away, there came a final dance with empty hands. At last the instructor, having nodded to the musician—who lowered his flute and took off his head-harness with a great air of relief–gave the word to dismiss.

Leon joined the others in the bath-room. Hippias kindly told him where to get some olive-oil, and handed him a box full of greyish powder; and then, seeing that he seemed rather lost, showed him how to oil his body and powder it and rub it until he was covered from head to toe with lather. Then he lent him a *strigil*, a curved metal blade fitted on a wooden handle, to scrape his body clear of the oil and powder and froth. Finally, the two cheerfully drenched each other with water, rubbed each other dry, slipped on their tunics, gave a small tip to the slave-boy who had watched the clothing, and, feeling very pleased with themselves, drifted over to a corner of the main hall where their elders were engaged in the favourite occupation of every Athenian, sitting about and talking.

No self-respecting athletic supervisor would be satisfied merely to provide training in gymnastics. He had also to give his patrons the other half of a good Athenian's education, music. This did not consist merely of singing or the flute and other instruments; it also included recitals from Homer and the other great poets, and it provided opportunities for recalling the history of Hellas and for discussing public affairs.

Today they were discussing foreign affairs, the power of the vast Persian Empire whose king, Darius, was known to be hostile to Athens.

'It was because of the way we helped the Ionian Islands during their revolt,' someone explained. 'After their defeat at Ladé . . .'

('That's what the captain told us about,' Hippias whispered.)

'Great King reconquered them one by one. But what he couldn't forgive was when the Ionians burned his fine city, Sardis; and when he heard we'd had a hand in that he sent for a bow and shot an arrow in the air to call the attention of the gods. "Oh Zeus," he prayed, "grant me vengeance on those Athenians!" And to this day one of his slaves has orders to remind him three times at every banquet: "Oh Great King, remember the Athenians!" '

'That's the sort of enemy we've roused against us,' the speaker ended very seriously. 'One who never forgets—and never forgives.'

But Leon and Hippias were too excited over the day's events to worry about the Persians: Great King was far away and the next day's training was very near.

The Physician and the Philosopher

Hippocrates is remembered as the greatest ancient doctor and is often called 'the father of modern medicine'. He lived during the fifth century before Christ, and with his students and fellow doctors he wrote a great number of books on medicine, including descriptions of diseases and case histories. Although his knowledge has been out-dated by the immense advances in medical science that have taken place since the seventeenth century, he is still considered to have set the example of the ideal physician as a man who is wise and kindly and has a deep respect for his patient and strong sense of duty. The 'Hippocratic Oath', a code of behaviour to guide doctors in their work, is still quoted in many medical schools when new doctors qualify. A few lines of it run as follows: 'The treatment I adopt will be for the benefit of the patient to the best of my ability and judgement, and not for his hurt or for any wrong. I will give no deadly drug to anyone even if he asks for it nor will I recommend this. Whatever I hear or see of people's lives, whether I am attending the sick or not, I will keep entirely to myself, regarding the information as a sacred secret.'

Hippocrates spent much of his working life on the Greek island of Cos, where many sick people came to visit him. In the following excerpt he is visited in Cos by one of the great philosophers of his day, Empedocles, who is suffering from a painful disease which he has tried in vain to cure in semi-magical ways. Empedocles himself had a reputation for curing people, and here we see how different was his approach to illness from that of Hippocrates.

The Physician and the Philosopher

When Hippocrates reached the enclosure it was the hour for the gymnastic class, and over the *palaestra* wall he heard the familiar piping of a flute and the singsong sound of his brother's voice.

'Up and down, over and back, up and down, over and back.' Through the half-open door he could see naked bodies, sweating faces, swinging arms and legs glistening in the sun, row after row of men, old and young.

Sosander caught sight of him and came lumbering out, dressed only in a short kilt. He wiped the sweat from his forehead with the back of his hand, and looked at his younger brother with affection.

'You know that you have a distinguished visitor?'

'Yes, I've been told so. Is he here already?'

'Yes. Podalirius is with him, but I fancy he finds it difficult to pacify the great man.'

'Why has Empedocles come here?'

'I do not know. He would not talk to me. But I watched him, and I should say that he is suffering from backache, although he tried to move as though he were young and healthy. Even the greatest of men, unless they die young, must some day stoop to an aching back!'

In the courtyard outside his consulting-room Hippocrates found two handsome slaves, elegantly dressed. They were of equal height and had the yellow-gold hair of the people from the north. He looked at them with interest.

'Are you twins—identical twins?'

'Yes.'

'Your master is inside?' They bowed together, an identical bow, with the pride of those who know they serve the great.

Hippocrates' consulting-room was large, and was lighted by a high window as well as by the door. In his own chair he found a man sitting rigidly erect. He had a large head with a high forehead. His hair and pointed beard were white but carefully trimmed, his face strong and handsome. He held up a hand in greeting, but he did not rise. He wore an enormous purple sapphire ring on his thumb; the cloak on his shoulders was of the same colour.

Podalirius was standing beside him. 'Empedocles has come to consult you,' he said, with a note of irritation. 'He does not wish to discuss his affairs with me. He has tried all the chairs and finds none to suit him, not even yours, in which he is sitting now.'

Podalirius left the room abruptly. Empedocles waited until the heavy door curtains had closed before he spoke.

'Do you know who I am?'

'Yes,' Hippocrates replied. 'You are the son of Meton of the city of Acragas on the Island of Sicily, grandson of the Empedocles who won the chariot race in the Seventy-first Olympiad. Twice your native city has offered you the crown and would have made you king. Twice you refused the crown. What more would you have me know?'

Empedocles leaned forward, but as he did so, he stifled a groan. 'Forgive me for not rising at your entrance. I am having a severe attack of pain and I did not care to make a confidant of your assistant. Oh, o-o-oh!' he exclaimed. 'It is my back and my leg.' His face was drawn with pain and he gripped his thigh.

'I have cured others,' he panted, 'but I cannot cure myself.'

Sympathy showed in Hippocrates' eyes and he spoke quietly, 'Do you want to consult a man as young as I?'

'Yes, though you are even younger than I expected. I must put my cure in your hands. I have no choice.'

Hippocrates smiled faintly, and, drawing up the bench, he sat on the opposite side of the table. 'Tell me, then, what is your complaint?'

'There is a discord,' Empedocles replied, 'a strife between the elements within my body. You have but to bring these four basic elements that are in me, even as they are in all the universe, into harmony and you will cure me. Then I shall leave Cos singing your praises among the Greeks in every city of the civilized world.' He stretched out his hand and the purple sapphire flashed. 'Beyond that I shall tell the story in strange lands where men live who have never heard the name of Homer, nor listened to his harmonies, if men they may be called.'

Hippocrates waited, knowing that an ailing physician is sometimes the most difficult of all patients, and that the control of question and answer in any interview is an art in itself. Every experienced physician discovers that it is only the very young who come to him simply. Others bring their mistrusts and theories with them, and thus strive, unwittingly, to lead him away from what may be the simple truth.

Hippocrates leaned back and shook his head slowly. 'Here

in my *iatreion* you are not Empedocles the philosopher and poet. You are not a physician nor a god, not even a hero. You are a man in pain, asking for help.'

He picked up a reed pen, opened the inkpot, and pulled a small sheet of papyrus towards him. 'I am not interested in your hypotheses, not now. Talk to me as a little child. If you will do that I will try to help you. Not otherwise. Now! Let me ask the questions. Where does it hurt? When did it begin? What were you doing when you first felt it? What movement makes the pain worse?'

Empedocles heaved a sigh. 'Very well, I am a boy again.'

Hippocrates worked at his clinical problem with concentration, making occasional short notes. During the physical examination Empedocles began to talk again, but his examiner was stern and just a little angry, so he subsided, and the examination was completed in silence.

At last Hippocrates laid down his pen and smiled. 'Now you may speak.'

Empedocles began as though floodgates had been opened. 'I should have told you that the colour on my cheeks is not natural. For over a month I have used pigments such as women apply when age has stolen beauty away.'

'Yes, I recognized that as I entered the room.'

'One thing more,' Empedocles continued. 'I am thin, thinner than my wont.'

'Yes,' Hippocrates said gently, 'I know, The skin of your abdomen is relaxed and wrinkled, like a half-empty wineskin. Your loss of weight must have taken place very rapidly since the onset of winter. The evidence is all too plain.'

Empedocles nodded, and Hippocrates continued. 'Let me describe the future for you as clearly as I can, so that you will not reproach me in days to come or say that I was ignorant of your condition. You have pain in back and leg. You find comfort only when you sit erect or stand carefully. There is no trouble that I can discover in the leg itself.

'My conclusion is that you have a malignant disease of the spine. I can feel a lump low down, and the muscles of your back are in constant spasm.

'Now, it is possible that we can cure this disease for you by hot baths, the application of mud, skilled massage, and by extension of the spine on a bed which we shall build for you from an oak plank. My brother Sosander is expert in such matters. It might be that our treatment will succeed. I urge you to live in the light of that hope. In any case, I am sure we can help the pain. But if this disease is too malignant to yield to such treatment, then, Empedocles, there can be only one outcome.'

The two men looked at each other. 'You believe I will probably die?'

'Yes.'

Empedocles' face had turned grey round the artificial colour on his cheeks.

'How long?'

Hippocrates threw out his arms. 'The gods know. Four months, perhaps.'

Empedocles made a little moan and turned away. 'It is as I feared. Thank you.'

His voice sounded strange and high. Silence followed. Finally Hippocrates said gently, 'You must rest now, and you may want to bathe. Following that, I hope you will do me the honour of dining with me, and after dinner you will join me, I hope, in a short symposium with my assistants. Later we will discuss your treatment when we meet as usual in the garden. Treatment will bring you great relief, whatever the outcome—I'm sure of that.'

Empedocles looked down at the folds of skin that hung

pitifully on his wasted paunch. Then he rose slowly and drew himself up as straight as his back permitted, and clapped his hands to summon his slaves.

Hippocrates left the room while the twin slaves entered and began to dress him. They went about their task with swift, sure movements. A soft woven chiton was drawn over the master's head and a jewelled girdle fastened in place. His white hair and beard were combed carefully, and perfume was blown on the pointed beard. At last a small bronze mirror was produced. He looked and nodded, and so, at last, the purple mantle was placed on his shoulders and the slaves withdrew.

When Hippocrates returned Empedocles was sitting on the bench. He looked up and said solemnly, 'No man outside your circle must know that I have suffered pain or weakness. If I am to leave this body it must be with dignity. My followers are many. Let no man say he saw me in defeat. If, in the end, you cannot cure me, I will ask you to help me quickly out of this life. If Empedocles is to become no more than a memory, let it be a noble memory.'

Hippocrates slipped his hands under the old man's shoulders and helped him ever so gently to his feet. Empedocles took his arm, and they walked slowly across the square and into the house. There Hippocrates urged the patient to lie down and rest on his own bed. There was a rather weak protest at first, but finally Empedocles heaved a sigh and obeyed.

The two men had dinner alone, although Hippocrates' mother, Praxithea, came and went, helping the servant and frequently stopping to talk. When they had finished the men went out into the garden while the central courtyard of the house was prepared for the symposium to follow. A single tall palm-tree grew in the centre of the court, on which the rooms of two floors opened. The court was of such a size that when couches were placed round the four walls, each with a little stool for a wine-glass, it was ready to accommodate the ten asclepiads and Empedocles, with only one man to a couch. Praxithea had a table placed in the centre of the court beside the trunk of the tree, and on it a skin of Coan wine, a decanter of water, goblets, and a large black bowl, beautifully decorated in red with figures of the heroes of Troy.

When Praxithea sent out word that all was ready the guests came in and Hippocrates assumed the rôle of symposiarch, pouring wine into the large bowl and diluting it with water until he considered that the strength was suited to the level of conversation desired.

' "Wine is wont to show the mind of man," ' he quoted as they took their places, and Dexippus, as the youngest asclepiad, handed a brimming goblet to each man, beginning with Empedocles and circling to the right according to long-established rule. They laughed and talked.

Empedocles was brilliant and entertaining, while Sosander and Hippocrates vied with each other in carrying the conversation to many topics and to cities and people all round the Greek world. Empedocles sat upright on the edge of his couch, smiling a little ruefully at those who lay at ease, half reclining on the pillowed benches.

The symposium ended with the music, and the physicians crossed the open square and took their usual places beneath the plane-tree. Hippocrates called on his brother Sosander to open the discussion, and Empedocles listened.

'I know the meaning of back pain all too well,' Sosander said. 'It was for that very reason my father sent me, with my crooked back, to Thrace to be treated by Herodicus and to study with him as well. Now, thanks to his gymnastics, I am cured.

'Pain in the back can be treated by strengthening the

muscles and producing better body posture. Pain in the back when it is accompanied by pain in the leg as well is best treated by stretching the back in various ways. My preference is to lay the sufferer on a ladder and tie his feet firmly, but with great attention to comfort, to one of the rungs, then to raise the ladder gently and place it against a wall so that he hangs head downward. That is most effective, since the pain in the leg is caused by spine pressure, and stretching the spine relieves that pressure.'

Empedocles had been listening uneasily. He now made a gesture of distaste, and Hippocrates intervened quickly. Hippocrates was opposed to many of the well-known doctrines of Empedocles, and he wished to avoid a clash at this time and in this place before his disciples. Empedocles believed in magic. He believed that the sacred disease, which Hippocrates had discussed with his followers only the night before, was the work of a demon; that man breathed through the pores of the skin; that life and health could be understood only in relation to some hypothetical explanation of the whole of nature.

'We know,' Hippocrates said, 'that Empedocles, who is our guest this evening, is a great philosopher, and we hope that at some other time he will discourse on those things that interest him most. But here, by tradition and by rule, we confine our attention to practical medicine. We aim to aid the healing processes within the body and thus to relieve pain. This we will do for you, Empedocles, when you return to the *palaestra* to-morrow.'

'A thousand thoughts come crowding into my breast,' Empedocles exclaimed, and placed his hand on his heart. 'Here in the blood that surges round this thumping heart of mine, here it is that a man's thoughts arise, not in the brain as you have been taught. Egypt's Secret Book of the Physician, written long, long ago, begins with these words: "Everywhere he feels his heart because its vessels run to all the limbs."

'Surely you have seen, before the altar of a god, the cloud of vapour that issues forth with the blood when the god's priest plunges his long knife into the heart of a sacrificial animal? That vapour is the spirit leaving the body. It is starting on its long journey before rebirth in the body of another animal or man. Even the Hebrews, whose holy book has been read to me, have always known that a man thinks with his heart. Where else can our thoughts be, then, but in the blood?'

Hippocrates scowled, and his lips compressed themselves into a straight line. But Empedocles, seeing that a storm was about to break, changed the subject abruptly, with a mischievous twinkle in his eye.

'Let me tell you my story now. This pain began quite severely while I was on a secret journey to my former home in Sicily. For almost a month I suffered and remained in hiding, hoping to be better. Then my enemies discovered my hiding-place, and I escaped on a donkey, disguised as an old woman, and accompanied only by my twin slaves. I thought if I must die anyway, Mount Aetna would be a suitable place, and I knew my enemies would be waiting for me in the seaports.

'When I reached the top of the peak and looked down into Aetna's fiery crater life seemed suddenly sweet to me. I decided to escape death there if I could, and to go for help to the temple of Asclepius in Epidaurus. Friends brought me word then that I was being followed up the mountain. So I left my golden sandals and my purple cloak there on the crater's brim, and I hid myself. My pursuers came and took back word that I was dead, carrying with them the shoes and the mantle for evidence.

'So we escaped and took ship to Epidaurus. I went to the

temple to offer a sacrifice and I bought an ox, but it came unwillingly to the altar. That is a bad omen. The beast's bellowing protest echoed through the shrine until the priest could bury his long knife in the flank and the river of blood flowed out across the marble. I gave orders that the whole animal should be laid on the altar of Asclepius. I took no part away with me. I added a gift of gold to the god as well. I bowed down before the statue of Asclepius and touched his staff, and the snake that coils about it, with my hand.

'The Chief Priest said, "Remain here now and you will be well." So I did all that he told me to do. I took treatments and baths. I stood outside the temple and drank the clear, cold water that gushes from the marble mouth of the son of Asclepius. But it was all to no purpose.

'I returned to the Chief Priest, and he said to me, "One thing more you must do. Sleep tonight in the temple portico. Dreams will come to you, and I will tell you the will of the god."

' "I will do as you say," I said to him, "but first answer this question. Many men throughout the world who have been cured by some physician send to you a votive offering of thanks to Asclepius, that through the hand of the physician the god has restored them to health. Who are those physicians whose skill leads men to thank the god? And who is the greatest of living physicians?"

'The priest replied, "We have just received from Perdiccas, King of Macedonia, a statue of himself because he was cured by a young asclepiad.[1] I have heard of him before—his name is Hippocrates, son of Heracleides, of the family of asclepiads on the island of Cos. He may be called, I think, the first physician in all Hellas!"

---

[1] *asclepiads*: the profession of doctor was often handed on from father to son. Such families were called asclepiads because they served Asclepius, the god of healing.

'And so that night I did lie down in the *abaton* of the temple portico, side by side with many others, to sleep the sacred sleep of Asclepius. Most of my companions seemed to sleep, but I could not, and I watched the temple priest make his rounds, stopping to talk with those who had slumbered. A large earth snake followed him, coiling along the terrace after him, and being fed from time to time.

'Finally, as light began to edge the east, and Orion slanted towards the horizon, I fell asleep. And I did dream, then, a strange dream.

'In it, I stood on a ledge of rock at the very peak of a mountain, and I knew I was close to heaven. Behind me I could hear the bells of grazing flocks, a lovely harmony of sound that told of the valleys of men.

'Before me, and over a precipice, I looked down into the sea, far, far below. I was terrified and tried to shrink back, but I could not, for I found I was bound with ropes. Then I understood. This was the moment that must come to every man. My own life was behind me; the gods above and death before and below.

'But as I waited there, bound and helpless, a man came between me and the precipice. He held a long knife in his hand, like the knife the priest had plunged into the heart of the ox. And the man said to me, "I am Hippocrates of Cos," and with that, he cut the ropes that bound me. I felt the side of the knife blade cool and comforting against my leg, and the pain was gone.

'Slowly, delightfully, I wakened. Then I started up, for over my leg, where I dreamt the knife blade lay, the great earth snake was slipping, cool and smooth. The priest was standing a little way off in the shadow of the portico, watching.

'I told him my dream. But he shook his head and went away. Later in the day the Chief Priest sent for me, and said,

"It is the will of Asclepius that you should go to Hippocrates for help."

'So I sent a messenger to Aegae, to the King of Macedonia, and when the messenger returned he told me that you, Hippocrates, had gone back to your home in Cos. But he said that King Perdiccas was about to send his own ship to Cos with a message to you. Further, the king sent word that if I would join the ship in Piraeus I might make the last stage of the journey to Cos in it. That is how I came to arrive here in a Macedonian trireme.'

Empedocles looked about at the asclepiads mysteriously. 'There are others aboard the ship who have purposes of their own in coming here. Fame, among the Greeks, brings some men wealth; sometimes it brings them beauty, happiness. The captain of the trireme has a message for you, Hippocrates. Let some one meet him at the harbour in the morning.'

Hippocrates went with his guest as far as the shore of the sea and watched him ride away; a proud slave marched on either side of his donkey.

'There goes the man,' he mused, 'who would know all things by inspiration—always godlike whether in error or in truth. But he dreads the dark passage that lies before him now, as all men must. The boy within holds out a hand for help, and I, his physician, have so little to give, so much to learn!'

Death of Alcibiades

Alcibiades was wicked. He was the handsomest man of his time, a good athlete and brave soldier, a capable commander both on land and sea, a skilful politician, wealthy, charming and witty, but totally lacking in principles. He persuaded the Athenians to undertake a risky, ambitious but brilliantly planned expedition to conquer Sicily. They put him in command with two others, but then recalled him to stand trial for being involved in a scandalous prank which took place just before the expedition sailed, and of which he may or may not have been guilty, but which was only too much in keeping with his usual scandalous behaviour. He escaped from arrest, deserted to Athens' enemies the Spartans, and advised them how to ruin the expedition – and consequently Athens. He forfeited the good will of the Spartans by another scandal – he became the lover of the wife of one of the Spartan kings (they always had two kings at the same time) and he had to flee once more. The rest of his life was a series of daring exploits and clever intrigues. He became friendly with a powerful Persian who was governor of several of the provinces of the Persian Empire which were nearest to Greece; and the Athenians, in an hour of crisis, forgave him for a brief period and put him in command of their navy, in the hope that he would secure Persian help. As admiral he won several battles and temporarily restored the Athenians' chances of winning the war; but then one of his subordinates, rashly disobeying his orders, suffered a defeat, and the suspicions of the Athenians were aroused again. Alcibiades went off to live in a castle which he had managed to secure for himself near the Dardanelles – on the edge of both Greece and Persia where he could play the one off against the other. But then Athens lost her fleet in a disastrous engagement which took place quite near to Alcibiades' castle, and which would not have happened if the admiral in command had listened to Alcibiades' advice; and so Athens lost the war and had to surrender. By this time Alcibiades had many enemies among both Spartans and Persians who thought him too dangerous to be allowed to live. He was assassinated when on his way to the Persian Court, hoping to charm and influence the Great King of Persia himself. The following excerpt from Peter Green's story about his life tells how this happened.

Death of Alcibiades

When Pharnabazus received Lysander's instructions, he sat a
long while in troubled thought, his wine untasted, the peacock
fans nodding gently above his head in the tireless hands of his
slaves. Then he sent attendants to command the presence of
his half-brother Bagaeus and his uncle Susamithres. They came
in together: lean and wiry both, dark-faced and hook-nosed,
the old and the young wolf. The Satrap greeted them formally,
but without warmth. In the labyrinth of palace intrigue it was
not wise to be over-familiar with one's kinsmen.

He gave Lysander's letter to his uncle, who read it through,
his face set. At the end he nodded, and passed it to Bagaeus.
Pharnabazus' eyes never left his half-brother. It is better that
he should kill for me, he thought, than sit here in the palace
with a hand itching at his sword-hilt.

Bagaeus said: 'It is easily done, my lord.'

'You may find it harder than you suppose. Alcibiades is a
brave man.'

'But he is alone.'

'No,' said Pharnabazus; 'no, he is not alone. The Arcadian

who came here with him still follows at his heels. And the woman Timandra also.'

'He is gone, then?' It was Susamithres who spoke.

'Two days since. I gave him letters and passports for all the provinces through which he must pass, and sent him to Susa to the King. Lysander's message reached me today.'

Susamithres and Bagaeus looked at each other.

'Perhaps I was not as foolish as you imagine,' said Pharnabazus gently. 'I think that Alcibiades might not have proved unwelcome at the Royal Court.'

'What message did he carry to the King?' There was an urgent note in Bagaeus' voice.

'He went to plead his country's cause. I suggested the arguments he should employ myself. The Spartans' power in eastern waters is altogether too strong for my liking.' Pharnabazus shrugged. 'The responsibility for what the King may hear will rest with Alcibiades alone. I shall disclaim any part in it.' He looked from one to the other of his listeners. 'I will confess privately that I find my present position somewhat embarrassing. The oaths of friendship I sealed with Alcibiades still hold good. He has been an honoured guest under my roof. I would be loath to betray the trust he has placed in me. Nevertheless, I cannot ignore this . . .'

'. . . Command?' there was a shade of scorn in Bagaeus' voice.

'Shall we say suggestion? I am a loyal servant of Artaxerxes. But at the same time my position here on the Hellespont is awkward in the extreme.'

Bagaeus rose to his feet. He seemed visibly relieved. 'In that case I do not think there is anything more to discuss,' he said. 'You may write to Lysander that your agents have left to do your bidding. We shall take horse today. You may depend on us to do all that is necessary.'

'I do not doubt you,' said the Satrap.

Bagaeus added suddenly: 'The woman Timandra that Alcibiades has taken with him. She is of noble birth, is she not?'

'She is,' said Pharnabazus. 'What of it?'

'Do her relatives approve of this liaison with a foreign exile?'

'You know our customs as well as I do. They cannot approve of it. But the girl is headstrong, and Alcibiades is ... Alcibiades. They have had very little choice in the matter.'

'Thank you,' said Bagaeus. 'That is all I need to know. We shall report to you again at the conclusion of our mission?'

It was a statement rather than a question. Pharnabazus inclined his head, and the two men went out quickly. Pharnabazus stared after them with troubled eyes.

The only light in the small room was a guttering lamp set in a bracket on the wall. The oil was bad, and the wick old: the flame spluttered and flickered, casting wavering shadows on the bare earthen floor, the open doorway where the curtains swayed in the faint night breeze. It was stiflingly hot; the air was full of the shrill piping of mosquitoes. Through the window the scattered lights of the village were visible in the blackness, and the sound of rustling leaves hinted at the trees and bushes which grew thickly round the house.

On the wooden bed Alcibiades lay in an uneasy sleep, sheepskins piled over him. The day after he had left Pharnabazus at Dascylium he had contracted a fever; and now he tossed and twisted, his thin cheeks flushed, sweat prickling out on his forehead. His hair had grown extremely long during the past year, and a grey lock fell across his face as he rolled over on to his side.

Timandra, sitting on a low stool beside him, watching every movement he made, stretched out a white hand and pushed back the tangled mass from his forehead. Then she dipped a cloth in a bowl of water that stood beside her, and gently wiped his flushed face. She was a girl of barely twenty, with the dark, classic features of the pure-bred Iranian. Yet her youthful face was strong and decisive; there was assurance as well as love in her black eyes and her aristocratic features bore an odd resemblance to those of Alcibiades himself. She was still dressed in the mud-stained habit in which she had ridden south that day over the rough roads of Phrygia; but the heavy pins that held up the braids of her hair were of wrought gold.

She sat motionless once more, her eyes fixed on the thin figure on the bed. He was quieter now; but his hands still plucked feverishly at the coverlets. His arms were bare, and the heavy muscles relaxed with his deep breathing. Her ears were strained for the slightest sound: the crackling of twigs, the distant barking of dogs. Several times she glanced towards the door, where the Arcadian sat outside in the portico, his drawn sword laid across his knees. A frown crossed her face. She was—though she did not admit it even to herself—both jealous and afraid of this strange silent man: his unwavering devotion was like a personal affront to her. Yet tonight he was a welcome presence. She felt danger in the air: the atavistic prickling of the spine that heralds pursuit.

Alcibiades stirred, groaned, and uttered a strangled cry in his sleep. She knew, without turning round, that the Arcadian had come in at the sound of it. She raised her hand in caution, and the boards creaked as he went back outside.

The heavy eyelids fluttered, then slowly opened. Two grey eyes, brilliant with fever, stared at her unrecognizingly. A voice that seemed to come from a great distance said: 'I've had ... the strangest dream ... Timandra ... can you hear me? I dreamt ... that I was dressed in your clothes ... that scarlet gown you wore when I first met you ... You were holding my head in your arms ... and adorning my face with

... with powder and paint ... I *saw* it all ... It was as if I were someone else ... looking on ...' He coughed, and sat up, shivering. Slowly his eyes cleared, and he took in the details of the squalid room. Timandra put an arm about his shoulders, and lowered him gently on to his pillows again. She poured out water in a pitcher, and he drank greedily, the drops spilling on to his naked chest with the trembling of his hand.

When he spoke again it was almost in his normal voice. He smiled weakly. 'I'm sorry,' he said. 'You have enough to trouble you without such fancies ...' He stretched out his hand and grasped hers.

She said in a low voice: 'I am afraid.'

'Afraid? Of your family? Of staying with me?'

She shook her head. 'No, Alcibiades. Never that. I chose to go with you knowing very well what it would mean. It is you I am afraid for. You can shake off the past from your mind like a dog coming from water. But it is still there. You can forget, but your enemies cannot. Whatever you do now, sooner or later they will hunt you down.'

He shook his head. 'Have you ever heard of Odysseus?' he asked. 'No: why should you? He was a king in Ithaca many years ago, and his enemies were more numerous than mine will ever be. Yet he came home in the end.'

'Home?'

'Why, yes.' He leaned on his elbow and quoted: ' "Be brave, my heart; you have endured worse things than this." ' He looked out of the window into the night.

'A south wind,' he said. 'We shall have good riding weather tomorrow. What is this village called?'

'Melissa.'

'How far is it to Metropolis?'

'Ten miles,' she said. Then: 'Did you hear something?'

'How nervous you are . . . What should there be to hear?'

'I don't know . . .' She got up and walked slowly round the room. 'It's past midnight,' she said. 'If you are well enough we can leave in four hours.'

'I shall be well enough . . . Drunk or sick, I can still ride a horse. Besides, after Metropolis the going will be easier . . .'

But she still paced, uneasily up and down.

'You must sleep,' he said gently. 'You have not slept since we left Dascylium.'

'Who will watch over you?'

Alcibiades turned his head towards the doorway. 'We are well protected,' he said.

Timandra hesitated for an instant; then she sat down beside the bed once more. Alcibiades turned over towards her, and after a little slipped into a fretful sleep. She bent over him gently and laid her head beside his, stroking his cheek with soft fingers. She did not hear when the Arcadian's sword slipped from his knees and clattered to the ground at his feet.

Alcibiades was the first to wake up, choking and coughing, the shreds of a confused nightmare still befogging his mind. The lamp had gone out and the room was in total darkness. Yet somewhere a reddish glow danced before his eyes, and when he tried to breath the air was thick and tainted. There was a roaring and crackling in his ears. Gasping, he flung off the coverlets and sprang to his feet. The acrid smell of burning timber came to his nostrils, and he stumbled blindly round the room trying to find the door. Behind him he heard Timandra cry out in terror.

His sword . . . where was his sword? He blundered into the

curtains and pushed through them, naked as he was, on to the portico. A blast of hot air hit him in the face, and the flames licked downwards from the roof. Through the smoke, in the light of the burning building, he heard a clamour of voices, and saw figures darting backwards and forwards in the brush-wood. Then he tripped against something soft; and looking down he saw the limp figure of the Arcadian, his limbs sprawling grotesquely, an arrow protruding from his throat. As he bent to pick up the sword that still lay beside the body another arrow whistled over his head and buried itself in the lintel of the door. The sword in his hand, he plunged back into the darkness of the house.

Timandra caught him by the arm. 'There's no other way out . . .' she began, and burst into fit of coughing.

He brushed past her into the bedroom. 'Get the bedclothes,' he called. 'As many as you can. Wrap them round your head and body. Keep close behind me . . .' He grabbed at a handful of blankets and thrust them into her arms. Then he found his cloak and swathed his body and left arm in it. Sword in hand, he ran down the steps on to the open ground, and the dark figures scattered before him.

Timandra, who had followed him closely, now twisted aside in the darkness and plunged unnoticed into the cover of the trees at the instant the first arrow hit him. She saw him halt in his tracks with a sharp cry of pain and put up his hand to his shoulder. Then the air hummed with the twanging of bow-strings, and she shuddered and covered her face with her hands.

He stood for an instant, silhouetted against the burning house, swaying on his feet. Then the sword dropped to the ground, and he collapsed and lay still. When at last the Persian archers came forward cautiously and gathered round him, they found fifteen shafts standing clear through his body.

From her place of concealment Timandra now saw two tall figures come forward into the light, and the archers make way for them. They stooped over the body for a moment, and then rose to their feet once more.

A young voice, harsh and expressionless, said: 'This is the man. Our task is done.'

'He died well, Bagaeus.'

'A fool can always die well.' The tall man seemed to hesitate. Then he observed: 'There's one dangerous tongue that can wag no longer.' He walked towards the house, shielding his face with his cloak. When he came back, he said: 'The other fellow is dead also. We have nothing to fear.'

'And the girl?' asked Susamithres.

'She's probably still in the house. In any case she knows nothing.'

With an incoherent cry, a man broke from the group and plunged desperately into the flaming building. Bagaeus watched him go unmoved. 'His daughter is hardly worth the fetching now, I should have thought,' he said.

Timandra sank to her knees half-fainting as shriek after shriek rose above the crackling of the fire. Then, abruptly, they ceased.

Susamithres said in an unsteady voice: 'Do you plan to go back to Pharnabazus now?'

'Most certainly. What danger is there? And besides ... Alcibiades was not the only one who needed ... watching. Yes, I think we should certainly return to Dascylium. In fact' —he paused as an idea struck him—'we might well make a gesture for the benefit of our Satrap. He has a suspicious nature. I should not like any doubt left in his mind that our mission has been carried out.'

'He won't thank you for that,' said Susamithres.

'Perhaps not. But Lysander will.'

He drew his long curved scimitar, and the blade gleamed red in the light of the flames.

'I shall take back some proof of this deed with me,' he said. He stepped forward, grasping the sword with both hands, and raised it high in the air. It took him three strokes to sever the head from the body of the corpse.

Then he picked it up carelessly by its hair and tossed it to one of the archers standing by. 'Pack that in my saddlebag,' he said, wiping the blade of his scimitar on a wisp of grass. 'And wrap it well. I dislike blood.' He turned to the silent group of men who had done his work for him. 'Well,' he observed, 'your family honour has been pleasantly avenged. Your sister is dead, and her father with her. I must thank you for the zeal with which you have done what I required of you.' He turned back to Susamithres.

'If we ride now we can be well on our way by daybreak,' he said. 'I don't think there is anything further here to detain us.' He walked away into the darkness. Susamithres beside him, their three attendants following close behind. One of these carried a blood-stained bundle. None of the rest moved or uttered a word till they were out of sight. From down the hillside there presently came the sound of hooves. Then these too died away into the distance. After a while the group of Persians silently followed them down the winding trail between the trees. The fire had not roused the neighbourhood; no one was stirring in the village.

Dawn was breaking when Timandra came out into the open and moved slowly towards the mutilated body of the man she had loved. The fire was dying down now. Only occasionally there would come a loud crack and a puff of smoke as charred timbers collapsed. Slowly the light spread over the hillside, and from the valley came the first faint sounds of morning. Then a slight breeze began to blow, barely ruffling the surface of the grass. Softly, imperceptibly, a fine cloud of ash was carried from the ruins and settled on the two motionless figures. When the sun rose above the trees it could not distinguish between them; for the living woman was grey with the greyness of the dead.

The war between Athens and her allies and Sparta and *her* allies came to an end with the blockade and surrender of Athens. It had been a long and bitter war and in the course of it there had been violence and revolutions in many of the cities which were involved on one side or the other. As a result many Greeks were left stateless and were eager to enlist as soldiers in the service of anyone who was willing and able to pay them. Ten thousand of these mercenaries were recruited by Cyrus (who was the younger brother of the Great King of Persia, and was governing the provinces of Asia Minor) under the pretence that he needed them as part of an expedition against some unruly hill tribes. He marched his army further and further into the Persian Empire until it was impossible to disguise from the Greeks any longer that he was aiming to attack and dethrone his brother Artaxerxes in his capital, Susa, which was beyond the Tigris and Euphrates rivers and for the Greeks terrifyingly remote from their Mediterranean sea. Having come so far they reluctantly agreed to go the rest of the way. In a battle fought at Cunaxa near Babylon, the Greeks utterly routed that part of Artaxerxes' army which was drawn up against them, but Cyrus got himself killed in an impetuous charge in which he nearly succeeded in killing Artaxerxes with his own hand. This left ten thousand Greeks surrounded by enemies— for the Persian part of Cyrus's army quickly melted away. In spite of both threats and deceitful promises they refused to surrender their arms and began to march towards their nearest hope of safety—the Greek cities on the coast of the Black Sea, some six hundred miles away. After several days' marching their commanders were treacherously lured away to a conference by the Persians and murdered. At first the leaderless Greeks were overcome by despair, but next morning they met together and elected new commanders, among them a young Athenian named Xenophon, who afterwards wrote the story of the whole adventure. Under their elected leaders the remainder of the ten thousand fought their way through mountains against fierce mountaineers, crossed wide rivers and snow-covered passes and finally arrived at the Black Sea some six months after the battle of Cunaxa, having lost only a few hundred men.

James Barbary, in *Ten Thousand Heroes*, describes how Leon, a Greek boy from Cos (the island where Hippocrates had once lived), who is apprenticed to a Greek doctor in the service of a Persian nobleman, makes friends with Nika, the daughter of an Armenian chieftain, who is escaping from slavery in a Persian household. Together they join the Greeks after the battle of Cunaxa and are able with his medical skill and her knowledge of the country to help them by making friends with some of the native peoples and acting as scouts.

The following excerpt describes the crossing by the Greeks of the River Centrites, which divided the territory of the fierce Kurdish mountaineers from the province of Armenia. The description of the crossing, apart from the personal adventure of Leon and Nika, follows very closely the description given by Xenophon himself in his own account of the expedition.

Between Two Fires

Next morning Nika demurely let Leon take the reins, and got up in her usual place behind him. The further northward they rode, the wilder and more rugged the mountains became, and again the bitter wind blew. By nightfall they reached a village on a mountainside, looking down on the river Centrites, that had not been lived in for years—evidently sacked and abandoned in some old frontier war.

'I wonder how Xenophon and his comrades have been getting on today,' said Leon as they dismounted amid blackened and tumbledown houses in what was once the village square.

Nika pointed back, the way they had come. 'Look—there has certainly been fighting. You see those birds in the far distance?'

Like far-off dots, swirling around the white peaks to the south, and ever and anon diving sinisterly, Leon could see vultures—eaters of dead flesh.

'Back in those hills—a great battle,' said Nika grimly. Turning to see where, below, the broad mountain-fed river Centrites tossed and foamed through its valley, Nika clutched Leon's sleeve. 'And ahead, Leon—look!'

The road down to the river was clearly marked. Facing each other on either bank were some miserable huts—sure signs of a ford, since human beings would hardly choose to live like that, on opposing river banks, unless they could communicate. Above the rushing torrent, strung along a range of heights, were horses and camp fires and armed men.

'Armenians?' asked Leon.

'Persians.'

'But how have they got there?'

'The Persians keep a governor hereabouts called Orontas. They call him Governor of Armenia—though his power does not run half a day's march into the mountains. The king no doubt sent word to him to oppose the Greeks, so he has gathered troops. Chaldeans—you can tell by their spears and long wicker shields. And Mardians. Now listen, Leon—despite what I said before, you and I must cross that ford tonight.'

'But you promised to wait three days.'

'I know. But as you see, those Persians and their mercenaries have only just come up. They've not yet posted sentries at the ford. By tomorrow, there will be patrols everywhere—blocking our only way into Armenia.'

'But, Nika, you gave your word—'

Yet Nika had so often been right, here in the mountains—and a physician might indeed live very comfortably up there with those Armenian tribesmen. But, Leon reflected, it would mean never hearing Greek spoken again, or living in a Greek way, speaking one's mind, electing leaders, exercising reasonable judgement. If one couldn't live like a Greek at least, thought Leon, feeling rather pleased with himself for such a solemn, important thought, one might as well die like one.

'Very well, Nika, go if you must,' said Leon in a more friendly tone, 'but I'm obliged to stay.'

'You see those vultures back there?' reiterated Nika fiercely.

'I tell you, Leon—tonight there is a chance. Tomorrow will be impossible.'

'One of two things is bound to happen, Nika,' said Leon, feeling this important argument had to be won, or he would never be able to look himself in the face again. 'Either the Kurds will defeat the Greeks. And when those Persians on the other bank get to hear, they'll go away. True? Or, what is more likely—Xenophon and the Greeks will defeat the Kurds. Our army will arrive here and chase off the Persians, as they have so many times before. In three days we shall know—and either way, we shall cross eventually.'

'I like Xenophon himself, and I certainly did give my word,' said Nika at last, though regretfully. 'Very well, Leon of Cos. But I still think you are foolish.'

That night the girl was unusually silent. They had decided not to risk a fire, and even in the shelter of those tumbledown houses the night was cold and comfortless. Towards daybreak, Leon awoke shivering—to find Nika gone!

Leon peered through the half-light in despair. Yes—Nika was nowhere to be seen—and she had taken the horse, too.

Leon felt bitter and sorry for himself. The Armenian girl had abandoned him. He was alone here amid hostile mountains, armed with only a dagger. If the ten thousand Greeks did arrive, well and good. But—if not?

Leon spent the most miserable two hours of his life, in wait, watching the Persians assemble their men on the far side of the river.

He was roused by the sparkling clatter of hooves over rock. Leon clutched his dagger, determined to sell his life dearly. . . .

Towards him came Nika, smiling broadly. Across her saddle-bow was hung the carcass of a young mountain deer, with tiny, tapering horns.

'Leon—see what I've brought down with my sling this time!'

Nika then noticed his stiff face and defensive gesture. 'Leon—did you really suppose I'd gone off and left you?'

'What else was I to think?' said Leon, ashamed of himself.

'But I gave my word. Since when has the word of an Armenian been worth less than the word of a Greek?'

There was nothing Leon could say.

Nika let the carcass of the young deer slide to the ground. 'Skin that for me—and I'll forgive you. Let's risk a fire, shall we? I'm hungry—and we might as well die full of hot meat, as empty.'

'Die?' said Leon, fumbling incompetently with his dagger. He found it much easier to dress a difficult wound than skin a dead animal—and Nika knew it.

'The Greeks are nearer than you think—but the Kurds are not defeated, either. They've moved back in their thousands—across the precipices we rode beneath yesterday. They have huge piles of stones, ready to hurl down on the Greeks—and hundreds of bowmen in ambush.'

'Can't we warn them?'

'Listen—it's already too late.'

Boy and girl paused. Faintly from the mountains was borne a cry that at close quarters all the Greeks' enemies had cause to dread—the *paean*, sung in attack. And louder, though still faint, the savage answering war cry of the Kurds. The battle had evidently begun.

The Persian camp across the river grew animated, and sent out extra patrols. They too had heard.

'We can but wait,' said Nika in a more friendly tone. 'Well, Leon—we might as well cook this meat. Let what may be our last meal be a good one. I shall now show you the way we Armenians roast our venison—'

About noon came a heartening sight—the first column of the Greeks! Dust-stained, many with fresh wounds, they marched down the mountainside raggedly, but with their heads held high. They made straight for the failing smoke of that cooking fire amid the ruined houses.

'Hullo, youngster!' cried a Rhodian slinger, out in front – Leon knew him well. 'Hullo, Armenian wench. Quick – give me some of that meat before the rest of the hungry devils arrive!'

During the next hour the entire Greek army came pouring in, hungry, battle-stained but triumphant. Foraging parties were sent out and came back after a while from neighbouring villages with meat, corn and wine. The generals arrived – and Leon sought out Xenophon, to explain why he had failed, not that it mattered now.

All this time, the Persians across the Centrites kept on watch. Though outnumbered, they were armed, fresh, and ready to bar the crossing of the river.

Towards evening, scouts of the Greek cavalry came up to Xenophon and Chirisophus, to say that the Kurds behind them, though routed in that day's battle, had once again re-formed their ranks. They were moving up behind the Greeks to renew the onset.

What Chirisophus the Spartan had dreaded was coming now to pass. Tomorrow, the Greeks would be caught between two enemy fires.

At dawn, all the generals of the Greek army met at a solemn sacrifice. By then the Kurds – a horde of wild, bearded, fur-capped barbarians – were actually forming up on the mountain behind, watching for their best chance to attack.

To Leon, the generals' conduct as the sun rose appeared strangely calm – to kill the sacrificed beast, inspect it for omens, roast it on the pyre, then partake of the ceremonial meal and offer the gods their rightful share – all with two enemies actually in sight. Today the omens – so the word ran round the watching army—were good. What was more, the rumour went that last night Xenophon the Athenian had had another of his prophetic dreams. In this dream he was fettered —and suddenly the manacles fell off of their own accord.

On the far bank of the river, the Persians and their allies watched sceptically from their entrenchments. Now and then a Persian archer would try his luck with a dropping shot. The whistling arrow would fly across the river in a high arc—and fall short. But woe betide anyone who came down to the river bank!

After sacrifice, the Greek infantry began cleaning and polishing their armour. If this were to be their last battle, at least they would look their best in the eyes of gods and men.

After giving some necessary orders, Xenophon sent for Leon and Nika.

'Well, Armenian girl—what do you think of our chances?'

'Well, Athenian—I think today you Greeks are going to be crushed—like a nut between the jaws of a nutcracker.' She pointed her right hand towards the Persians, her left towards the Kurds, and brought them together with a painful jerk, as if cracking a nut.

'You heard tell of my dream?'

'We Armenians would have given it a different interpretation. Listen, Xenophon—seriously. The fetters of life itself may drop from you today. You may find the release of which your dream spoke—in death.' However, Leon saw Nika as she uttered these gloomy words make with thumb and finger the secret sign that averts evil. Xenophon for a moment looked grave. Then with a smile he said, 'But the omens, too, were favourable.'

'What do you want us to do for you, Xenophon?' interrupted Leon.

'Quite a simple thing. Find me another ford.'

Leon was astounded. 'But isn't that asking the impossible?'

Xenophon shook his head. 'Men are creatures of habit. The road into Armenia has always gone by that ford down there. Who but men in a predicament like ours would bother looking for another? But if we go this time by the regular road—with Persians entrenched ahead of us and Kurds waiting their chance behind us—Nika's nutcrackers—it will be a massacre. So find me another ford.' Xenophon made the gesture of dismissal.

'But any living creature that walks along that bank,' grumbled Nika, 'will look in no time like a pin-cushion full of Persian arrows.'

Xenophon turned his back on them without another word. This gesture enraged Nika and Leon, and sent them off determined to find another ford just to spite him—which was what Xenophon intended.

Riding that horse—which by luck had not yet been claimed for the cavalry—the pair of them made a cast along the mountainside, up stream, well out of bowshot. At last they came in sight of another settlement—a couple of dozen mud-and-wattle houses, standing on the far bank of the river. On this side, facing, was a single tumbledown hut.

'Could that be another ford?' asked Nika in a whisper. 'Or is that one hut on our bank just coincidence?'

Leon dismounted. A fat woman with a pile of folded clothes on her head came out of one of those huts on the far bank. She walked towards the swiftly rushing river, and there Leon expected to see her go down on her knees and begin her family's washing. Instead she kirtled up her skirts and stepped into the swirling water. Nika gasped, as if sure the torrent would rise up to her chin. Instead the fat woman walked majestically onward, one hand crooked up to steady her washing—and in midstream the water scarcely came to her dangling girdle.

'There's your other ford, Xenophon!' exclaimed Nika. 'A miracle!'

This was an even better way across than the place the Persians had seized, by which all travellers passed—yet seemingly it was used only for crossing over to wash clothes on those flat stones near the solitary ruined hut.

'We must go back quickly and tell of this marvellous luck,' Leon told her.

'Start walking, then,' Nika answered, from horseback. 'Or run, if you like. I shall now ride across that ford and go on my way homeward. I'm taking this horse as my pay. Leon, why put your hand on your dagger, thus, and look so fierce? Are you hoping to stop me?'

'Nika—you would never betray us to the Persians?'

'Never. I hate the Persians worse than you do. Remember, it was Persians who enslaved me. Across that ford, in Armenia, I am completely free. I now wish for one thing only—to go quietly to my father's house.'

'And suppose your own people—the Armenians—decide to fight us. Would you help them—against the Greeks?' asked Leon puzzled and hurt by what he took to be Nika's desertion.

'Goodbye, Leon,' said Nika. 'You will never understand.' Astride the horse she reached down her hand for another of those curious handshakes—fingers grasping the offered wrist—with which she had first pledged her friendship.

'Goodbye, Nika,' Leon said, feeling gloomy and alone.

As she rode towards the river, he added in a loud voice, 'And good luck!'

Nika turned back once, to wave. Then the forehooves of her mount splashed into the river water. Leon watched Nika cross—a good ford indeed, the horse scarcely wet its belly.

Sad instead of triumphant, Leon tramped back to the Greek headquarters.

'Xenophon, just as you said—we found a good ford. Much better than the one over there. Only two miles upstream. But, Xenophon—Nika took the horse and went across the Centrites. She's gone to her father's house in Armenia—'

But Xenophon was grinning delightedly, only interested in the success of his plan.

He told Chirisophus the good news, and the two generals walked to and fro, their heads together, earnestly discussing how to get the army across. No army is more easily crushed than when crossing a defended river.

The plan they agreed on must have been ingenious, for when Xenophon called Leon to him again, he was smiling broadly.

'Leon—you are to take the wounded across—using the ford you so cleverly discovered—in the second wave, immediately after Chirisophus' heavily-armoured vanguard. That will be safest. By the way, there in the hills I organized that squad of stretcher-bearers we once talked about. You'll find them very useful.'

'And yourself, Xenophon?'

'Wait and see. You will get a surprise—and so will our enemies, Persian and Kurd alike. Though, alas, it will all have to be done without the aid of my little trumpeter.' Xenophon looked across the river towards the mountains. 'I'd hoped to make great use of her—over there in Armenia.'

Leon turned away, feeling peculiarly lost and alone now Nika was gone. The discipline and continual hard work of an army camp came as a shock, after their wild free ride through the mountains. Above all, these Greeks had devoted their lives to war—and Leon was sick of war, which had meant to him personally only hideous wounds to dress again and yet again; and too many times the dreadful sense of failure that comes to a physician when his patient dies.

Yet, when it came to the crossing, Leon from his safe vantage point on the far bank amid the wounded had to admire the military cleverness that Chirisophus and Xenophon showed in getting their army across.

It had all depended on that second ford – of which to begin with the entrenched Persians did not even suspect the existence.

Seeing the Greek army about to move, the bearded Kurdish hordes, clad in their furs and carrying their shoulder-high bows, all began to descend from the mountainside, ready for an onslaught.

The bulk of the Greek army – including Leon and the wounded – marching just out of bowshot, followed Chirisophus and the armoured vanguard upstream to the new ford. The Persians meanwhile raced parallel with them along the far bank, to keep them in sight.

Suddenly Xenophon and picked men of his rearguard turned back moving quickly – as if to cross at the old ford, and so take the hurrying Persians from the rear. This made the Persians hesitate, so Chirisophus successfully raced them to the new ford, and got across unopposed. His soldiers got wet to their thighs – no more. The bulk of the army's baggage was going over – when the wild Kurds came yelling down.

Xenophon at once wheeled his picked force about, and formed them up in battle line to face the Kurds – who came on confidently against this seeming handful of men in armour, now beginning to lower their long spears.

What counted was that bronze armour. Leon, looking from the safety of the far bank (for the Persians there had already been driven back by a charge from Chirisophus' men) knew by a tightening in his throat what Xenophon over there would do next. When the Kurds—fur-clad, a few wearing helmets, otherwise not armoured—came close enough for the stones they hurled to rattle on the Greek shields, out rang the first notes of the *paean*. That terrible battle line of Xenophon's, with spears couched, moved forward at a powerful rhythmical impulse which no troops in the world could withstand.

The Kurds fled—and before the first of them turned, to see what was happening next, Xenophon's men, retreating, had already reached the river bank and were going across, helter-skelter.

The Actor's Son

Mary Renault's book, *The Mask of Apollo*, is about the Greek theatre in the fourth century B.C. Through the mouth of Nikeratos, the tragic actor, she describes an actor's life as she imagines it, his travels and performances in the dramatic festivals round the country; and she shows something of the part played by the theatre in the lives of the Greeks.

A play was then not firstly an entertainment, but an offering to the gods; and this idea is conveyed throughout the book by the reverence Nikeratos feels towards his mask in which he plays the part of the god Apollo.

In the following passage Nikeratos tells of one of his early appearances on the stage, when he was still a child.

The Actor's Son

At three, I was Medea's younger son, though I can't remember it; I don't suppose I knew I was on a stage. My father told me later how he had brought home his Medea mask beforehand, in case it frightened me; but I only stuck my fingers through its mouth. It is hard to make actors' children take masks seriously, even the most dreadful; they see them too soon, too near. My mother used to say that at two weeks old, to keep me from the draught, she tucked me inside an old Gorgon, and found me sucking the snakes.

I do remember, though, quite clearly, playing Astyanax to his Andromache. I was turned six by then, for Astyanax has to work. The play was Euripides' *Women of Troy*. My father told me the plot, and promised I should not really be thrown off the walls, in spite of all the talk about it. We were always acting out such tales as a bedtime game, with mime, or our own words. I loved him dearly. I fought for years to go on thinking him great.

'Don't look at the Herald,' he said to me at rehearsal. 'You're not supposed to know what he means, though any child would that was right in the head. Take all your cues from me.'

He sent me out in front, to see the masks as the audience saw them. Climbing up high, above the seats of honour, I was surprised to find how human they looked, and sad. While I was there he did his part as Cassandra, god-mad with two torches. I knew it by heart, from hearing him practise. It was his best rôle, everyone agrees. After that he changed masks, ready for Andromache. This is the play where they bring her in from the sacked city on a cart piled up with loot, her child in her arms, just two more pieces of plunder. A wonderful bit of theatre. It never fails.

I was still small enough to be used to women's arms; it was odd to feel under the pleated dress I grasped at, the hard chest of a man, holding each breath and playing it out with the phrases, the rib-cage vibrant like the box of a lyre. If one thinks, I suppose most men's sons would die of shame to hear their father weep and lament in the voice of a woman. But as he never missed his exercises, I must have heard them from the first day I drew breath: old men, young men, queens and booming tyrants, heroes, maidens and kings. To me it was the right of a man to have seven voices; only women made do with one.

When the day came, I was still aggrieved there was no mask for me, though I had been told again and again children did not use them. 'Never mind,' said my father, 'the time will come.' Then he pulled his own mask down, the smiling face going into the solemn one. He was in the prologue as Athene.

Outside the parodos[1] the cart was waiting, drawn by four oxen, with the gilded spoils of Troy. At last came the call-boy, and my father in the pale mask of the shorn-haired widow. He clambered up, someone hoisted me after; he settled me on his knee, and the oxen started.

Out beyond the tall gateway was the great curve of the

[1] *parodos:* a side entrance onto the stage.

theatre. I was used to the empty tiers. Now filled with faces it seemed vast and unknown, murmuring and dangerous as the sea. My father's voice whispered, 'Don't look at the audience. You're scared of strangers. Think how they chopped up your poor old granddad. Lean on me.'

This is not how I myself would direct Astyanax. He is Hektor's son; I like him alert and bold, thinking no evil till the time. But my father knew his business too. Even the men were sighing, as we came slowly on into the orchestra; I could hear the little coos and cries of the women, floating on this deep bass. Suddenly it took hold of me. My father and I, by ourselves, were doing this with fifteen thousand people. We could carry them all to Troy with us, make them see us just as we chose to be. I can taste it still, that first sip of power.

Then I felt their will reach out to me. It was like the lover's touch, which says, Be what I desire. All power has its price. I clung to Andromache my mother and leaned upon her breast; but the hands I answered to were Artemidoros the actor's. As they moulded me like wax and sculpted us into one, I knew the many-headed lover had caught him too; I felt it through both our skins. Yet I felt him innocent. He did not sell, but gave freely, love for love.

The Herald came, with the news that I must die. I remembered I was not supposed to heed him; but I thought I should look sorry for my mother's grief, so I reached up and touched the mask's dead hair. At this I heard sighing and sobbing rise like a wave. It was coming from the block where the hetairas[1] sit; they love a good cry more than figs. But it was a few years yet before I knew to look for them.

When the Herald bore me off to die, I thought everyone backstage would be there to pay me compliments; but only the wardrobe-master's assistant came in a hurry, to strip me

[1] *hetaira:* a high-class prostitute—but see *Thais at Athens.*

111

naked and paint on my bloody wounds. My father, who had
exited soon after me, ran over to pat my bare belly as I lay,
and say, 'Good boy!' Then he was off; it's a quick change from
Andromache to Helen, what with the jewels and so on. It is
always a splendid costume, meant to show up against the
other captives'. The mask was most delicately painted, and
had gold-wreathed hair. He went on, and I heard his new
voice, bland and beguiling, answering angry Menelaos.

Soon after came my cue to be brought on, dead. They
stretched me out on the shield, and a couple of extras lifted
it. The day was warm, but the breeze tickled my skin, and I
gave my mind to lying limp as I had been told. The chorus
called out the dreadful news to my grannie Hekabe; lying,
eyes shut, while the Herald made a long speech about my
death, I prayed Dionysos not to let me sneeze. There was a
pause, which because I could not see seemed to last for ever.
The whole theatre had got dead silent, holding its breath.
Then a terrible low voice said just beside me,

Lay down the circled shield of Hektor on the ground.

I had been well rehearsed for this scene; but not with
Hekabe. I had nothing to do but keep still; and this was
Kroisos, the leading man. He was then at the peak of his
powers, and, fairly enough, did not expect to tutor children.
I had seen the mask, and that was all.

I had already heard him, of course, lamenting with Andromache; but that is her scene, and I had my own part to think
of. Now, the voice seemed to go all through me, making my
backbone creep with cold. I forgot it was I who was being
mourned for. Indeed, it was more than I.

No sweetness here, but old pride brought naked to despair,
still new to it, a wandering stranger. At the bottom of the pit
a new pit opens, and still the mind can feel. Cold hands touched

my head. So silent were the tiers above us, I heard clearly, from the pines outside, the murmur of a dove.

I was not seven years old, I think I remember; but no doubt I have mixed in scraps from all sorts of later renderings, by Theodoros or Philemon or Thettalos; even from my own. I dreamed of it, though, for years, and it is from this I remember certain trifles, such as the embroidery on his robe, which had a border of keys and roses, glimpsed between my eyelids. When I think of these dreams it all comes back to me. Was it Troy I grieved for, or man's mortality; or for my father, in the stillness that was like a wreath of victory on Kroisos' brow? All I remember for certain is my swelling throat, and the horror that came over me when I knew I was going to cry.

My eyes were burning. Terror was added to my grief. I was going to wreck the play. The sponsor would lose the prize; Kroisos the crown; my father would never get a part again; we would be in the streets begging our bread. And after the play, I would have to face terrible Hekabe without a mask. Tears burst from my shut eyes; my nose was running. I hoped I might die, that the earth would open or the skene[1] catch fire, before I sobbed aloud.

The hands that had traced my painted wounds lifted me gently. I was gathered into the arms of Hekabe; the wrinkled mask with its down-turned mouth bent close above. The flute, which had been moaning softly through the speech, getting a cue, wailed louder. Under its sound, Queen Hekabe whispered in my ear, 'Be quiet, you little bastard. You're dead.'

I felt better at once. All I had been taught came back to me. We had work to do. I slid back limp as his hands released me; neatly, while he washed and shrouded me, he wiped my nose. The scene went through to the end.

[1] *skene:* the stage scenery (a wooden wall at the back of the stage with columns and doors for entrances and exits).

> *In vain*
> *we sacrificed. And yet had not the very hand*
> *of God gripped and crushed this city deep in the ground*
> *we should have disappeared in darkness, and not given*
> *a theme for music, and the songs of men to come.*

As the extras carried me off in my royal grave-clothes, I
thought to myself, surprised, '*We* are the men to come.' As
well as everything else, I had been responsible to Astyanax.
His shade had been watching from the underworld, hoping I
would not make him mean. What burdens I had borne! I
felt I had aged a lifetime.

My father, who had been standing behind the prompt-side
revolve and seen it all, ran up as they slid me off the shield,
asking what had come over me. If it had been my mother, I
dare say I should have raised a howl. But I said at once,
'Daddy, I didn't make a noise.'

Kroisos came off soon after, pushing up his mask. He was a
thin man, all profile, like a god on a coin except that he was
bald. When he turned our way I hid behind my father's
skirts; but he came towards us, and fished me out by the hair.
I came squirming; a disgusting sight, as you may suppose, all
smeared with blood-paint and snot. He grinned with big
yellow teeth. I saw, amazed, that he was not angry. 'By the
dog!' he said, 'I thought we were finished then.' He grimaced
like a comedian's slave-mask. 'Artemidoros, this boy has
feeling, but he also knows what he's about. And what's your
name?'

'Niko,' I answered. My father said 'Nikeratos'. I had
seldom heard this used, and felt somehow changed by it. 'A
good omen,' said Kroisos. 'Well, who knows?'

The Machina

The second of our two passages from *The Mask of Apollo* tells of
Nikeratos' determination that the play must go on, for the god's sake,
even at the cost of life itself.   The setting of the passage is Delphi,
a small town in the centre of Greece situated in spectacular mountain
scenery (see *Death at the Crossroads*, p. 21). It contained a shrine in
which the god Apollo was thought to prophesy through the mouth
of a priestess called Pythia (see *The Sybil*, p. 177).

It contained a theatre and also an arena for the Pythian games –
only slightly less important to the Greeks than the Olympic games.
It was popularly thought to be the centre of the whole world.

The Machina

Our next engagement was at Delphi.

Anaxis was full of this prospect. With every year as his hopes in the theatre fell, he went further into politics, scouting out the land; and he had got wind of this booking from afar. The reason for a play being put on outside the festivals was to entertain the delegates at a peace conference, a very big affair.

Peace of some sort was overdue; for some years artists had had trouble in getting about at all, what with Spartans marching on Thebes, then Thebans marching on Sparta. Everyone was for Thebes in the early days. But since all her victories, the old neighbourly jealousy had waked up in Athens; and we had an alliance with Sparta now. I suppose this was expedient, but it disgusted me; it is things like this which make a man like me leave politics to the demagogues. The one good thing was, that those dour-faced bullies needing to ask our help proved they were down to third rôles for good and would never play lead again. They had been thought invincible, only because they were in war-training from the cradle to the grave; but the Great War went on so long that other Greeks too got this professional experience, though against their will. By the end of it a good many had borne arms since they were boys, and barely knew another calling. So, like actors short of work, they went on tour. There were still nearly as many wars going on as drama festivals; and all of them needed extras.

No sooner had the Spartans been put down, than the Arcadians, who had been content till now with fighting here and there for hire, thought to try ruling the roost on their own account. So the Peloponnese was full of smoke and soldiers, just when it had looked like a good season with clear roads.

Most other cities, however, had had enough. Hence this peace conference at Delphi.

Ask some poet to describe the awe of Delphi, and some philosopher to explain it. I work with the words of other men. I looked back down the valley, the olives winding and falling mile on mile to a rock-clipped blink of sea. Beyond a vast gulf of air were the highlands of Mount Korax, cloud-patched with sun and gloom; westward the iron cliffs of Kirphis; above us reared Parnassos, more felt than seen. Its head was hidden by its knees, the rock-towers of the Phaidriades, which themselves seemed to gore the sky. Truly, Apollo is the greatest of all chorus-masters. The town, with his temple in the midst, is tiny as a toy in all this vastness; yet all those titan heads seem to stand around that and look towards it. They are the chorus round his altar; if he raised his arm they would sing a dithyramb. I don't know any other deity who could bring off such a show. At Delphi, you don't ask how they know it is the centre of the earth.

I looked up the great steeps of the Phaidriades, which stand behind the theatre like a skene reaching to heaven. 'Look!' I said. 'Eagles!'

'My dear Niko, they are as common here as doves. Do let us get to the inn while they have something left to eat. If this is your first visit, you need not tell the world.'

Next morning we looked over the theatre. We were pleased to find not a bit of obsolete equipment anywhere; after the big earthquake of five years back, they had had to refit completely. There was still scaffolding round the temple, and the roof a makeshift of pinepoles and thatch; Apollo and the Earth Snake kept up their ancient war. We shouldered back through the town under the tall proud statues, past the treasure-houses for the cities' offerings, Anaxis waiting patiently while I tipped the guardians and gaped at all the gold. We squeezed past sightseers and guides and pilgrims, soldiers and priests and slaves, temple-sweepers with brooms and whores with fans; stalls selling lamps, ribbons, raisins, books of oracles, and sacred bayleaves for lucky dreams. Looking up and about, I thought it was like dwarfs playing on a stage designed for titans. I suppose it was still a small, solemn place when Xerxes' army came to lift the gold, and they asked Apollo what to do. 'Get out,' he said; 'I can take care of my own.' They still show the rock-peak he hurled down on the Persians, blazing aloft the Phaidriades and yelling through the thunder. I bought, for keepsake, a little gilded bronze of the god drawing his bow. A pretty thing. The old statue in the temple, that is an Apollo to shoot straight. But the shops don't copy it now; they say it is crude, and art must move with the times.

Presently came a slave to meet us, bidding us take wine with our choregos.[1]

We were led to a fine painted house beside the Stadium, and saw at once that our sponsor was a syndicate. Three were Delphians; but by watching whom everyone looked at first, we guessed it was the fourth who was putting up the money. He was one Philiskos, an Asian Greek from Abydos. What

[1] *choregos:* the man who supplied the money for a stage performance, and got much of the glory if it was a success.

with his clothes and his ivory fly-whisk, and Delphi being as full of gossip as a winter hive of bees, we added two and two. This was King Artaxerxes' agent, playing host to the Conference with Persian gold.

While sweets and civilities went round, we discussed the play. The citizens of Delphi weren't mentioned from first to last; it was the delegates who must be pleased. It was my turn to direct and choose a rôle, and I had proposed *Hippolytos with the Garland*. It was as good as settled, when some little man, who I'll swear only wanted to go home saying he had spoken, said it might give offence to the Athenians, by showing King Theseus in the wrong. We both assured them it was revived in Athens about one year in five, and was the surest hit in repertory. Too late; the damage was done, the panic started. At a peace conference, it went without saying that everyone would be looking for slights and insults. *Helen in Egypt* might affront the Pharaoh; *Medea* the Corinthians; *Alkestis* the Thessalians. Once or twice I stole a glance at Anaxis, meaning, 'Let's leave them at it; before they miss us we'll be in Thebes.' But he had set his heart and hopes on this production. When I whispered, under cover of all the dickering, 'Try offering them *The Persians*!' he looked down his nose and would not laugh.

From mere boredom I started dreaming; and dreams bring memories. Next time they paused to scratch their heads, I said, 'Why not *The Myrmidons*?'

How often, if ever, you have seen this play depends upon where you live. It is a favourite in Thebes and well liked in Macedon. In Athens it is hardly ever revived; no sponsor likes to take the risk. Ever since Aischylos' own day, some people have always disapproved; and you never know when they will get on the judges' board. Demagogues have proclaimed that the love of man for youth is a relic of aristocracy (a politician will say anything, if it strikes where he wants to hit), and the last thing they want to hear is that the play is noble. They would rather those great avowals did not ring on so in the heart.

Today, however, it turned out to be just the thing. Having looked at it backwards, sideways and upside down, they could not find a single slur on anyone's ancestors, gods or city.

We went our way, stuffed full of Persian sweets and almonds, cursing the waste of time but satisfied with the outcome. Anaxis was content with his rôles. I, being protagonist, would do Achilles; but Patrokolos has some lovely lines, and so has Briseis later. Krantor would do Odysseus and the other odd parts, 'and,' said Anaxis, "I suppose Apollo in the prologue?'

Walking as we talked, we had come out on top of the theatre seats, and were gazing over the temple roof at the mountains. I said, 'No, I'll take Apollo myself.'

Anaxis raised his brows. 'Do you want to? It's a very quick change. Don't forget Apollo is flown on; you'll have the harness to get rid of.'

'I've a fancy for it. One's not in Delphi every day. Call it my service to the god.'

That evening we were summoned back to meet the chorus-master, the flautist and the skene-painter. The painter, Hagnon, was an old friend from Athens. Between rehearsals, I stayed to chat with him while he painted trophies-of-arms on the reveal and Greek tents on the flats. From time to time he would shout for his man to bring him ladder or paint, or shift his scaffolding, complaining that the fellow was never at call. He was lanky and spindle-shanked, with a straggling yellow beard; once I caught him staring at me, and it stirred some memory I could not place; but it was clear he would stare at anything rather than work, and I thought no more of it. Hagnon had had to take him on at Delphi, having come to do murals in a private house and getting this contract afterwards.

Rehearsals went smoothly. The chorus of Myrmidons were fine well-built men and could sing as well. I found a saddler to make me a flying-harness. The crane-man weighed me for the counter-weight; finding him skilful, I only did my fly-in once with him, and rehearsed the prologue from the god-walk.

I enjoyed working on *The Myrmidons*. I had steeped my soul in it when young, and it still moved me. I have heard Patroklos better done; Anaxis had technique enough to sound young, but fell short of charm; still he did bring out the character's goodness, without which nothing makes sense.

Delphi was filling up every day. Delegates were arriving; and, as Anaxis told me, all kinds of agents to watch the delegates, sent by the opposition in their various cities, their secret allies in rival cities, the interested kings and tyrants, and I don't know whom. I was more amused by the high-priced hetairas who had come in from other towns and set up house to the rage of the Delphi girls; they would make a better audience than all these peace-traders. Leaving Anaxis to smell about, I went walking on the thymy hillsides or through the olive groves, hearing for chorus the cicadas and mountain birds, while I ran over this speech or that. One day Anaxis came bustling up to say that the envoy of Dionysios had come at last, and bettered our hopes by being some great personage and the tyrant's kin. My mind was on the placing of a breath-pause, and the name went straight out of my head.

At my request, Hagnon was painting the masks for the principals; the local mask-maker was fit only for chorus work. but Hagnon worked wonders with his carving as a good painter can. He had done me a fine Achilles, and was working on Patrokolos. The Apollo was not yet carved.

Ever since Lamprias died and his widow sold up his things, I had kept the mask of Pheidias hanging, in a box like a little shrine, on the wall of my room in Athens. Remembering Phigeleia, before every contest I would wreathe it and make some offering. There was no good reason why I should have brought it with me—one can always find a friend to mind one's things when touring—yet some reason had seemed good, and it was on the table at my lodging. That evening, when the lamp was lit and the shadows moved with the flame, it seemed to look straight at me with eyes inside its eyeholes, as if to say, 'Nikeratos, you have brought me home. Dionysios' winter reign at Delphi is past and gone. Have you not heard my music on Parnassos? I should like to smell skene-paint again.'

It gave me a start. I sat down at the pinewood table, chin in hand, as my father taught me to do before a mask, when one wants to think oneself into it.

'Glorious Apollo,' I said presently, 'are you sure? Wouldn't you like your face to be more in fashion? You could have anything; a solid gold wreath, jewelled earrings; it's nothing to the backers here. And they'll be at the dress rehearsal.'

A night breeze blew in from the heights of Korax; the lamp-flame quivered; Apollo looked at me with dark lidless eyes. 'At Phigeleia,' he said, 'you promised to give me something. Have I asked for anything before?'

In the morning, I took it to the light. The paint was dull and worn, but the carving perfect. Hagnon was in the theatre, touching-up; I opened the box, and asked him what he thought.

He looked long in silence, frowning and biting his lips. I waited for him to say the usual things: stiff, harsh, primitive. But he looked up as if some pain had gripped him, and said, 'Oh God, what was it like when men had certainty like that?'

'God knows,' I said. 'I'll wear it and see what comes to me. Can you repaint it?'

'Oh, yes; of course. I can touch it up and tone it down,

till from in front you'd hardly tell it from a modern one.
Listen, Niko. I'll buy you a new one and paint it free. Just
give me this and we're square.'

'No; I meant can you do it as it was?'

He lifted it out, turning it in his hand and scratching the
paint with his finger. 'I can try,' he said, 'God help me. Leave
it with me.'

'Well,' I thought, 'I've looked my last on him now.' Which
indeed was true.

Next day Hagnon did not come to the theatre. Someone
said he was shut in his room and would not open; he did not
sound sick; he must have company in bed. At evening, he met
me in the wine-shop. 'The paint's not set,' he said, 'but come
and see.'

He had propped the mask on a table with a lamp before it.
I gazed in silence, while the eyes of Apollo Longsight, full of
unplumbed darkness, stared out beyond us. We had served
his turn. He had come back to his mountain lair, like a snake
in springtime, to have his youth renewed.

My long quiet made Hagnon uneasy. 'The room's too small.
I should have shown it you in the theatre.'

I said, 'Did you do this, or did he do it himself?'

'I'll tell you what I did. I found it was a day for the
oracle; so I sacrificed, and took this with me, and went down
to the cave.'

I stared. He looked rather shamefaced. 'It was just to get
the feel. But one must ask something, so I asked which attributes the god's face should show; and the Pythia answered—
quite clearly, I could hear it without the priest interpreting—
"Pythian Apollo". So I went home and started work.'

'Apollo Loxias,' I said. Before, rubbed down almost to bare
wood, it had seemed to show only the Olympian, balanced and
clear. But poring in the faded lines of mouth and eye and

nostril, Hagnon had found lost curves and shadows. A shiver ran down my neck. Here was the Double-Tongued, whose words move to their meaning like a serpent in a reed-bed, coil and counter-coil; how can a man tell all his mind to children, or a god to men?

Presently I asked Hagnon what the Pythia had been like. He answered, 'Like weathered rocks. She had lost her teeth, and under the drug she dribbled. But the fact is, I didn't look at her long. In the back of the cave, behind the tripod, is a crack running into the darkness; and in its mouth is a seven-foot Apollo cast in gold, with eyes of lapis and agate. It must go back beyond the Persian Wars; it has that secret smile. I couldn't take my eyes from it. But I heard what she said.'

I sent out for some wine, and tried to make him take the price of his time; but he said it would be bad luck. Before we drank, we both tipped our cups before the mask.

I asked him why, if these old forms moved him so, he still worked in the current style. 'Just put me back,' he said, 'in the glorious age of Perikles, and dose me with Lethe water, to unknow what I know. Once men deserved such gods. And where are they now? They bled to death on battle-fields, black with flies; or starved in the siege, being too good to rob their neighbours. Or they sailed off to Sicily singing paeans, and left their bones there in sunken ships, or in the fever swamps or the slave-quarries. If they got home alive, the Thirty Tyrants murdered them. Or if they survived all that, they grew old in dusty corners, mocked by their grandsons, when to speak of greatness was to be a voice from the dead. They're all gone now; and here are you and I, who know just what became of them. What will you do with that mask, Niko, when you have it on?'

'Well may you ask. At least I'll play in Aischylos, which is what it was made for. Perhaps it will teach me something.'

125

The lamp smoked, and Hagnon trimmed it. As he pricked up the wick, there was a flicker on the face of Loxias, and it seemed that the dark side smiled.

At dress rehearsal, just as I had foreseen, the sponsors asked Hagnon why he had fobbed them off with old stuff repainted. When he showed that he had not charged for it, they said, amazed, that they had ordered everything of the best. This mask lacked grace and charm; it was too severe. Sponsors are sponsors, so I did not ask them what Apollo needs charm for, coming to tell of doom in words like beaten bronze. Instead we said the god had chosen this mask expressly, through the oracle, for his Pythian likeness. That kept them quiet.

When these fools had gone, Gyllis the Theban courtesan —getting on now, but still famous for her verse-readings— came round to kiss us all. She had been in front, and vowed we should make a hit. Mikon the mechanic, who loved his work, asked if I found the crane run smoothly. 'I like an artist to feel secure, or he can't do himself justice. Here in Delphi, we never make an old rope do. Twice for a man, once for a chariot, that's my rule. The last play was *Medea*, so you get a new one.' I assured him I had not felt safer in my mother's arms; and he scrambled back into his wooden turret with his oil-flask and his crock of grease.

That evening it rained, which damped our spirits; but day broke cool and blue, with barely a breeze. When we got to the theatre, the upper tiers were full, and the sponsors' servants were fussing about the seats of honour with rugs and cushions. Through the cracks in the skene, it looked like a real occasion. I stripped for my flying-harness, and belted over it Apollo's white, gold-bordered tunic, while my dresser worked the harness ring through the slit.

On my table stood the mask in its open box. From the mask-maker I had bought it a new, fair wig. It was young, strong hair, such as the peasant girls sell when they have to cut it for mourning. The life of the face flowed into it; I pictured it streaming from the head of the furious god, while his arrows clattered at his back with his angry strides, as he came down the crags like nightfall to the plain of Troy. That is the Apollo of *The Myrmidons*; straight from Homer.

I lifted my hands palm upward, asking his favour, and then put on the mask. As the dresser arranged the hair, the flutes and kithara began, and Mikon from his turret signalled 'Ready'.

I ran out, waving on my way to Anaxis, who was kissing Anthemion for luck, and to Krantor strapping on the corselet of Odysseus. Behind the back of the skene-room was the hidden platform, with Mikon's boy waiting there to hitch me on the crane-hook. The music rose, to cover the creak of the machine, the rope at my back went taut. I grasped my silver bow, and leaned on the harness in the arc of flight.

Up I soared, out above the skene; the crane-jib, with its travelling screen of painted clouds, lifted and turned upon its pivot. The sea-sound of voices hushed; the play had started. Above the Phaidriades an eagle wheeled and cried, balanced like me upon the air. The jib slewed up and outward, and the music stopped for my speech. It was then I felt, quite close above me, a twang in the rope, and a slight sag down. A strand had parted.

At first I thought it must be just a jolt of the pulley. Mikon was trustworthy and the rope brand-new. I resolved to think no more of it. I was about one-third through, when I felt something go again. No doubt this time. I felt it strain and part; I sagged down a good inch.

. . . Zeus' battle-shattering aegis . . .

I could hear myself going on; while quick as a heart-beat the thought ran through me, 'A notched rope—Meidias. Thirty feet down, on stone.'

When the tawny eagle with his stallion crest
Swoops down, safety is hard to find ...

Wise words. It was still coming out of the mask, one line prompting the next. Two strands gone, how many left? The last taking all my weight could not last long. If I called out now, they might just get me back in time.

For I am Phoibos, zenith-cleaving, sun-shafted archer,
Unforsworn tongue of truth ...

Brave words. I could hear myself as I spoke them, breaking off to yell, 'Help! Help! Let me down!' and the theatre echoing with a belly-laugh that would sound in my ears if I lived to threescore and ten. And it might be still too late. What a way to end, bawling like a scared child on a swing; what a line to be remembered by. The eagle circling the crags gave a long shrill 'Yah!'

I thought of the mask I wore. I had sat so long before it, I knew its face like my own. I thought of that human bleat coming out of it. And I thought, 'My father would have gone on.'

This had passed in moments. My voice still spoke the lines; now I put my will to them. The words, the light, the rock-peaks seen through the mask-holes; the smell of the mask, old and woody, mixed with new paint; the scoop of the hillside filled with eyes, struck on my senses clear and brilliant, as each moment passed which might be the last of my life. A kind of ecstasy, such as I have heard men can feel in battle, flowed all through me.

Suddenly the audience had got restless. There was a buzz; then someone shouted aloud, 'Watch out! The rope!'

It had started in the side-seats where they could see behind the screen. I wished they would keep quiet. I might be dead before the end of this speech; they could at least attend, not interrupt with stale news. I lifted my hand palm out, Apollo commanding stillness, and threw in the first tag I thought of, 'Lord of all gods is Fate!' Then I picked up the speech again.

Dead silence now. Each word dropped into a breathing stillness. In the harness-straps I felt a tremor and strain from the rope above. The third strand was parting.

It went. The fourth must be the last, I thought; it was giving already; I was sinking down. Then as the audience groaned with relief (or else with disappointment) it came to me what was happening. Mikon had been warned; he was paying-out softly, letting me down on stage.

One moment, it seemed, I was dangling from death's forefinger; the next my feet touched ground. It was over. The silence broke then. Here I was right downstage, with nobody to unhitch me, and they expected me to stand there taking bows. I got my hand back and slipped the ring, and made some kind of exit. My last line was about flying back to high Olympos. I had just enough sense left to cut it. With a keyed-up audience, it would have been the very thing for a laugh.

By now it seemed I had been up there by myself for days. It was quite strange to have everyone grabbing me backstage and asking me how I felt. 'Later,' I said. 'Just let me change.'

Anaxis rushed up to me, his boyish Patroklos mask shoved back, his beard and eyebrows staring; he had gone quite pale. He pushed a wine-cup at me, but after one swallow I put it by; I was afraid of throwing up. 'Can you go on?' he asked. 'Would you like Anthemion to stand in for you?' I pulled my face straight just in time. 'No, thank you. In the name of the gods, get out on stage; nobody's there.'

My dresser unharnessed me, and strapped on my panoply for Achilles, clucking and chattering. Mikon came running, the frayed rope in his hands, waving it about. 'Later,' I said.

Achilles has a good while to sit sulking, before he consents to speak, which would give me a rest; but when he does break silence, he has got to be worth hearing. My blood was still stirred up, I felt ready for anything; I remember thinking, 'This is just how one feels when acting badly.' However, when I got to the lines where he chooses glory before length of days, suddenly a burst of applause broke out and stopped the play. I had never thought of that; I think it was the nearest I got to losing my lines.

At last it was over. The noise seemed to last for ever. Even after I went to change, I could have taken another call; but of a sudden I felt hollow as an emptied wineskin, sick, and deathly tired. Even the applause seemed empty; it would have been the same for some juggler who had jumped through a ring of knives. I thought with loathing of my performance, which I was sure had been ham all through. Stupidly I stood while my dresser stripped me, trying to be civil to the people who had come behind. Presently Mikon brought his rope again, and showed it round.

'I checked it overnight, every foot.' He pushed it under the nose of two sponsors, who had come behind to complain. 'Look here, at the cunning of it. The strands were opened, and a hot iron laid inside. With filing it would have frayed, and I'd have seen it as I ran it out. This was done in the night. That drunken loafer, the painter's man, I'm told that he was seen here.'

Hagnon said, 'I saw him, round about midnight. I thought

nothing but that he'd picked up some odd job. Well, I hope
they find him. The young men were off on the mountain trails;
they reckoned he might have gone up there, to watch it
work.'

'Maybe.' I could not feel concerned. Near by was the bier of
the dead Patroklos; I pushed off the dummy corpse, glad of
something to sit on.

Krantor said, 'Where's that wine-jar?' He poured, and held
out a cup to me. I would have swallowed anything; but the
rich Samian fragrance told me this must be the best in Delphi.
It ran through me like new warm blood.

Anthemion tittered. 'It's a gift from some admirer in the
audience. It came round before the end of the last chorus;
the message just said, "To honour the protagonist". But you'll
be hearing his name, I'm sure.'

I put it down. 'You fool! Someone's just tried to break my
neck; and now you give me wine from you don't know who.
I wondered if I ought to take an emetic. It seemed less trouble
to die.

'No, no, Niko.' Old Krantor patted my shoulder. 'Drink it
up, my boy, I saw the slave who brought it. Groomed like a
blood-horse; born and bred in good service, that one. It must
come from a sponsor.' He looked at the two who had come
behind; but they coughed and looked elsewhere.

He filled my cup again. The wine, though neat, was so
smooth it went down like milk. On an empty stomach—I can
never eat before I play—I pretty soon felt the difference. I
started floating on air, needing no crane. Everything was
golden, everyone kind and good and beautiful. I turned, the
cup in my hand, and saw on my table the mask of Apollo,
propped in its box. My dresser had plaited the hair and bound
it, as I had shown him, in the style of Perikles' day. As the
wine lighted me up, it seemed about to utter prophecies. I

swayed to my feet before it. It was never I who had made that speech; the mask had spoken, I thought, while I hung like a doll in Apollo's hand. I tilted the cup, and poured him a libation.

Death of Philip

The father of Alexander the Great was Philip I, king of Macedon from 359 to 336 B.C. He was an ambitious soldier and fine general who during his reign conquered the whole of Greece. But he was also an awkward moody man and, like Richard I and Henry V of England, was apparently never satisfied with what he had won. After his conquest of Greece he started preparing a great expedition against Persia, the greatest power of that time.

Alexander did not get on well with his father and when Philip, ruthlessly following his own fancy, chose to divorce Alexander's mother, Olympias, and marry another woman called Cleopatra, Alexander and Olympias went into exile. Philip had offended other important people besides and some of these now began to plot his death. We cannot be sure to what extent Alexander himself was involved or even precisely aware of what was happening, but he was certainly prepared to take over the kingdom after Philip's death. As soon as he had secured his position he was quick to reorganize the kingdom and then to carry out his father's plans for the expedition to the East.

In Maurice Druon's book the plot against Philip's life is led by Pausanias, an army general, and described by Aristander of Telmessus, a priest who has the confidence of Philip. Alexander has returned from exile. The expedition is ready to sail. But before it leaves Philip holds magnificent celebrations for the marriage of his daughter to the king of Epirus, and Aristander consults the auspices.

Death
of
Philip

Alexander had just turned twenty. A month later, Philip's new wife was brought to bed of a son. He was called Caranus, from the name of a distant ancestor of great prowess of the kings of Macedonia. Philip thus showed the importance he attached to his birth; he did not conceal his joy and there were many indications that he already meant to give the new-born child a favoured place among his heirs.

The year of waiting I had imposed on Alexander was coming to an end. I feared that impatience and the birth of this small rival might lead him to commit some folly.

'You are separated from the throne only by the thickness of a breast,' I said to him. 'Destiny is on the march. Leave the gods to act.'

The marriage between the King of Epirus and Alexander's sister was due to take place in a few days' time.

Pausanias, however, was going about all over the city and, since his affair had been noised abroad, he spoke of it to every-one he met. Repeating time and again the story of the out-rage, he took everyone to witness how ungrateful Philip had been to him. Did not such a betrayal deserve vengeance? How much longer must Macedonia suffer so corrupt and base a king, totally subject to a woman's domination?

He found Olympias receptive. The fallen queen was sympathetic and encouraged his resentment. She let him understand that she would be far from ungrateful to anyone who would deliver her, by some happy accident, from her unfaithful husband. People do not speak of murder in precise terms, but hints can be dropped that make it clear enough. The ambitious Pausanias was intoxicated with dreams of redressing the wrong he had suffered and fused his own dishonour with all the resentments of the kingdom. He went to Alexander and, to test the prince's feelings, implored his counsel, asking him on whom and by what means he could avenge the affront. Alexander merely replied with the line from Euripides' tragedy of *Medea*: 'And the author of the wedding, and the wife, and the husband.'

By this he meant to anyone who wished to understand, Philip, Cleopatra and Attalus, who had contrived the union, as Creon had married his daughter to Jason, and made him repudiate Medea.

To gain importance both in his own eyes and in others', Pausanias, having consulted the princes, wished to take the opinion of the sages. He went to ask the advice of the philosopher Hermocrates, who had a school in Pella and was extremely hostile to Philip, on the best means by which a man might leave his name to posterity. Hermocrates looked the young man up and down, judged him for what he was, and replied to his secret thoughts by saying: 'He should kill the person who has performed the greatest deeds, and thus whenever that person is spoken of he, too, will be remembered.'

After that, it was not difficult to convince Pausanias that the act he was contemplating was also demanded by the gods.

Philip was not altogether unaware of the strange behaviour of the young officer of his guard, since rumours had reached as far as Athens that an attempt on his life was being prepared. There was nothing to prevent Philip having Pausanias arrested and thrown into prison; but Philip despised the author of his danger. He showed that surprising heedlessness of conquering kings towards the hidden perils that surround them when they are approaching their end. They disregard all warnings, refuse to appear to doubt their luck or to fear for a life they have hazarded so often; a blind, unconscious force drives them, when destiny has run its course, to measure themselves for a last time against fate and to walk, as if of their own will, towards the grave.

Philip had determined to make the marriage of his daughter to his brother-in-law of Epirus the occasion of great rejoicings as a prelude to his expedition into Asia and that the amplitude of his power might be displayed; he had even decided that the wedding should be celebrated in Aegae, the ancient capital, where the kings of Macedonia had their necropolis. In returning to the sacred city of his ancestors, he was drawing nigh to his tomb.

A fortified town, set on a rock dominating the valley of the Axius, a wild, magnificent site among lakes and forests, Aegae took on its forgotten life for a few days. From beyond Olympus, whose summit could be seen on clear days, ambassadors had come from every part of Greece, bearing presents for the bride and bridegroom and for Philip himself. The envoys of princes, republics and colonies had made the journey together with a host of priests, poets, actors and athletes from every land. The choice of Aegae was, moreover, a clever one on Philip's part; the new queen, Cleopatra, not yet risen from child-bed, could not leave Pella, and Attalus was on the Hellespont. Thus Philip could make it seem as if he were quite reconciled with his Epirus relations. Olympias was at his side, and so was Alexander.

On the first day, the ceremonies proceeded as arranged; after the consecration of the marriage in the temple, each ambassador came to present his gifts. The Athenian delegates, representing the most important city of the confederation, came forward last and their spokesman, while presenting the king with a gold crown from his fellow-citizens, read the decree which had been voted in his favour:

'We, Athenians, in token of the esteem and respect we feel for Philip, son of Amyntas, King of Macedonia and Hegemon of the Hellenes, declare that whoever should conspire against his life will be declared a traitor and an enemy to the cause of Greece. If the criminal should seek refuge in Athens, we hereby promise to deliver him up to the justice of Macedonia that he may be punished according to the customs of that country.'

Philip's face grew dark as he listened to the decree. The Athenians were really too solicitous. Was his death being spoken of so openly that his allies wished to show themselves innocent of a conspiracy that they were perhaps encouraging in secret? Demosthenes could not have been sincere in voting for this decree.

As on every important occasion, the oracle of Delphi had been consulted. And the messenger came to make public the Pythia's reply as interpreted by the priests of Apollo.

It read: 'The bull is garlanded; his end draws near; the sacrificer stands ready.'

Which might plausibly be taken to signify that the King of Persia was threatened with a great defeat, that the sacrificer was Philip, and that the expedition into Asia Minor would be victorious. And this was how the oracle was officially interpreted amid an appearance of great satisfaction. But to anyone who knew that Philip, sybaritic, sensual, opinionated, loving life and dominion as he did, came under the sign of the Bull and knew what sign succeeded to the Bull, and that Alexander was marked by Ammon the Ram, the oracle could assume a very different meaning. And Philip was seen to pass his hand several times across his brow as if he felt weary and anxious.

At the feast which followed, Philip asked Neoptolemus, the great Athenian actor, who was among the guests, to recite a poem. To flatter Philip in his military ambitions, Neoptolemus chose a passage from a tragedy which announced the forthcoming death of a conqueror reigning over a vast kingdom. And Philip was once again seen to pass his hand across his bandaged eye; then he glanced at the doors, as if wishing to assure himself of the presence of his guard. Pausanias, a short sword at his belt, was standing a little way behind him.

Olympias, her huge, metallic eyes shining with a beauty that time had altered but little, gave no sign. Alexander was equally impassive.

That evening, Philip told his friends how weary he was. Was he still young enough to undertake this great campaign? He was heard to talk of rest, of the pleasures of living at peace among happy subjects and a united family. Was it because he had married his daughter that he felt a certain melancholy as all fathers do in the circumstances? He tried to laugh at himself. But anxiety gave him a restless night. The next morning, before going to the stadium where he had organized games, he gave special orders for his security. He wanted to walk alone in the procession, apart from all the members of his family and suite, protected solely by an escort of his guard. Soldiers were to line the way to keep the crowd at a distance.

The tiers were already full of spectators when the royal procession arrived. Coming from the covered passage that led into the stadium the first to appear were the King of Epirus and his bride; acclamations greeted their entrance. Then, received with still louder applause, came Olympias, laden with gold ornaments, and Alexander in a green tunic which made his red hair flame. When passing through the long, dark passage, they had recognized Pausanias who, dressed in officer's armour, was commanding the guards spaced at intervals of five yards along the wall. He appeared calm and merely attentive to his duties. Then some little time elapsed. From every tier in the stadium all heads were turned in the same direction. The soldiers were dressing their ranks amid a clank of arms. The musicians were awaiting the signal of the director of the games. The King of Macedonia, the Hegemon of the Hellenes, had entered the stone passage.

I was not in the stadium that morning. About an hour earlier I had gone to the temple. There, I asked the sacrificer on duty to give me a mina[1] of virgin wax and prepare me a chicken; and I went into a chamber of meditation as if to take the omens.

I spread the virgin wax on the stone table in such a way that it formed a triangle whose base was towards me and whose apex was towards the stadium. From the opened stomach of the chicken I withdrew the entrails and placed them on the virgin wax, keeping them at the base of the triangle. I invoked the sacred names with the proper intonation and rhythm, repeating them the appropriate number of times, till I felt as if I had quitted my own body, had ceased to occupy the envelope of the flesh and could transport my strength to another place and into another person.

I waited for long minutes, my eyes fixed on the chicken's entrails, and finally in their pearly contortions, I saw what I expected to see. I saw the entrance to a tunnel, and Philip approaching the tunnel and, in the shadow, Pausanias. The images were small but precise.

[1] *mina:* a measure of weight (about fifteen ounces).

I began pressing the entrails of the chicken between my hands so as to make them spread upwards over the triangle of wax.

Meanwhile, first in a murmur, then in an increasingly loud voice, I directed the movement of the two men into whom I had transported my presence and whose image I was following on the pearly surface.

And when the viscera were compressed into the point of the triangle, I cried: 'Strike!' while squeezing with all my strength; and there was a great glow in which I saw the flash of a weapon, then shadow; the entrails had burst, covering my hands with gall and excrement.

I suddenly felt exhausted, as if my own life were departing, as if I were at once the murderer in his anguish and terror and the dying victim.

I opened my hands to outline on the stone table above the wax the shape of a new triangle, open at the top, so that the energy which had just escaped from one body might pass at once into another and that the liberated power might be received by him who was to make use of it.

When I rose to my feet, my legs were trembling under me. One is never certain of having succeeded. I wiped my hands, went out on to the parvis of the temple and looked towards the stadium. From the great clamour that came from it, I knew that Macedonia had changed its king.

The first shouts were taken by the more distant spectators for acclamations and a great ovation rose from the tiers of the stadium, wishing long life to the man who had just died. Then, suddenly, cries of horror took the place of joy.

Philip had not emerged from the passage. Shadow is propitious to crime. Within the covered passage, the king's body lay, his beard in the dust, his tunic stained with scarlet above the heart, and the porous stones were absorbing his blood. In his fall, his bandage had come undone, revealing the old wound of Ammon.

Some soldiers of the guard had set out in pursuit of the murderer. Pausanias, fleeing towards the exit, had gained a start on them and the cries of 'Stop him! Stop him!' proved ineffectual. His horse was tethered by the reins to the wall of the stadium; he had time to mount it and set off at a gallop; but he was caught by the low branch of a tree, which he had failed to see; it took him in the chest, and he fell to the ground.

He who is to die, and is blinded by some alien power, may have calculated every detail of his escape; but he fails to see the branch stretched across his path. Before Pausanias, stunned by his fall, had time to get to his feet, his pursuers were on him and a dozen swords pierced him.

Alexander lost not a moment in showing himself a king. He called Antipater to him, assembled the generals and counsellors, not to consult them or have himself recognized as sovereign by them, but to give them orders as a master and as if there were no question about it; and they all obeyed him without argument.

Philip's body was taken to the palace and that of his murderer hung on a cross in the middle of the square to remain there till the funeral.

Olympias left for Pella that very day with an escort. She arrived at nightfall, after a long ride on horseback, and went straight to the room of Attalus' niece. She found her still in bed, still weak from childbirth, her dark hair spread over the sheets. She untied her scarf, handed it to her rival and said: 'You can hang yourself, our husband is dead; if you have not the courage, I can call the guard.'

And she left Cleopatra alone behind doors barred with

spears. A few moments later, as there was no sound, they opened the doors and saw the young woman's body hanging from the wall, her face blackened and her tongue hanging out. Then Olympias ordered that little Caranus should be brought to her; she took up the baby, who was only a few days old, and whom they had wished to make a rival to her son; escorted by her entourage, she went to the temple of Ammon, had the fire on the sacrificial altar stoked and threw the child on to it as an expiatory victim.

At Aegae, the following morning, the gold crown the Athenians had sent Philip was found placed on the head of the crucified man.

Then the solemn obsequies were held; the priests advised that, to appease the gods, the bodies of both Philip and Pausanias should be burned on the same pyre; and their mingled ashes were placed in the royal necropolis.

Relations between the sexes differed in Greece from one city to another and from one period of time to another. It is difficult to form an exact picture of the treatment of women at Athens, but evidence suggests that they were expected to spend most of their time in their homes (unlike the men, who in the daytime congregated in the market-place, the sports grounds and other public places). They were not educated except to be literate and to look after their households – this would include the slaves (they would not have more than one or two, except for the very few whose husbands were rich). As a result they made dull companions for the witty, lively Athenian men; so among these passionate homosexual relationships were common. However there was a class of women who had more stimulating company to offer than the Athenian housewife. These were women (mainly Greeks from other cities) who set up as courtesans, were often well-educated and intelligent as well as beautiful, and sometimes attached themselves to an Athenian citizen in as lasting a relationship as the marriage which was forbidden to them as foreigners. Such was Aspasia, the mistress of the Athenian statesman Pericles. One of the most famous of the courtesans was Thais, who – so we are told by certain rather gossipy and not very reliable ancient authors – was a woman of remarkable gifts, and was allowed to accompany Alexander's army when he conquered the Persian Empire. She is said by those authors to have eventually married one of Alexander's generals, Ptolemy. After Alexander's death, Ptolemy seized Egypt, made himself king and founded a dynasty whose last queen was that Cleopatra who was loved by both Julius Caesar and Mark Anthony. The novel from which these excerpts come recounts the adventurous life of Thais. The first excerpt tells how she began her career at Athens.

Thais
at
Athens

The old man, feeling sorry for her, took her to her destination, a large stone house on the road that led from the Peiraic Gate to the *agora*.[1] Thais climbed down, thanked him and started toward the servants' entrance at the rear. She shook her head in exasperation, retraced her steps and raised the ornamented brass knocker at the front entrance.

After a long wait, an elderly eunuch, whose short robe emphasized his paunch, opened the door and examined her critically. 'What do you want?'

'I wish to see Ariadne,' Thais replied.

'We're making no additions to the serving staff at present.' He started to close the door.

She flung herself against it. 'I'm not a servant, and I've travelled a great distance to see her!'

The eunuch rubbed his bald head, stared at the intense girl and then led her to an inner court. 'Wait here,' he said, 'and I'll find out whether she'll receive you.'

[1] *agora:* the city centre. An open space surrounded by colonnades. There public meetings were held, market stalls were set up, and people met to talk business or gossip.

147

Thais looked around and clasped her hands in ecstasy. Columns of shining marble, elaborately carved at the top in the Corinthian manner, supported a roof of stone, and in the centre of the court was a water-filled pond in which lilies were floating. Torches set in gleaming metal holders provided light, incense was burning in a pot that was hanging from a silver chain, and standing on a rock in the pond was a stone lion whose mouth was open, water pouring out of it. Thais giggled. It was the first time she had laughed with pleasure since she had left Pella.

The eunuch returned, frowning. 'There are days,' he hissed, 'when Ariadne's moods drive all of us to distraction. Follow me.'

Thais walked down a corridor to a small chamber more beautifully furnished than any room she had ever seen. The walls were lined with thick, pure-white silk which hung in loose, graceful folds, a thick rug of the softest wool covered the floor and all of the furniture was covered with gold leaf. She was dazed for a moment, then became conscious of a woman with brown hair and kohl-rimmed eyes who was reclining on a divan, watching her.

Summoning her courage, Thais walked into the room and made a graceful obeisance.

Ariadne laughed, and her voice was husky, almost as deep and resonant as that of a man. 'I wanted to see the creature who threatened to tear Podeno apart.'

Thais laughed too. 'That was an exaggeration.'

'So I thought.' Ariadne laughed again. 'You're well-formed, but you're not a muscular girl.' Her manner became brisk. 'What do you want here?'

'I am Thais of Macedon, and even in my distant land, the great lords talk of the glorious Ariadne. I've heard it said that you accept girls for apprenticeship, and I've come to learn the arts of the *hetaerae* from you, if you'll accept me as a pupil.'

'How did you travel here?'

'I walked.'

'All the way from Macedon?'

'Yes, from Pella.'

Ariadne was astonished, then her painted mouth formed in a hard line. 'Are you sure you're not an escaped slave?'

Thais extended her right hand, on which she wore a small silver ring. 'If you can read the language of my people,' she said, 'you'll see it written here that I am a born freewoman.'

Ariadne inspected the ring and, satisfied, leaned back on her pillows. She dismissed the eunuch, who was lingering in the entrance, and studied the girl who stood before her. 'Obviously you have great perseverance, which is essential. And I'll admit you might be useful. Hellenes must become the intimates of Macedonians these days if we hope to survive. Do you know King Philip?'

'I worked for a time in his wife's kitchen,' Thais said frankly.

'No doubt you've heard that Alexander is going to visit Athens.'

It was difficult to control the excitement that welled up in her, but Thais shook her head and spoke calmly. 'I left Pella many days ago.'

Ariadne continued to scrutinize her. 'What talents entitle you to become a *hetaera* instead of a wench who finds her clients in the *agora*?'

Thais had anticipated the question. 'I believe I have many talents. I can read and write both Macedonian and Greek—'

'Who taught you?' The woman's tone was sceptical.

'My education was begun by my mother, who hoped I would rise higher in the world than had been possible for her. She was not a learned woman, but she gave me the tools, and after she died I always found ways to borrow books from the libraries of the lords who employed me.'

'It's odd that a girl from the hills of Macedon should have the desire to become a scholar.'

'I've never wanted to attend an academy.' Thais smiled. 'Ignorant women listen to the Oracle at Delphi or make sacrifices to the gods and watch for omens. But I prefer to remember the words that Aristotle spoke four years ago—'

'You're acquainted with Aristotle?'

'I was a serving maid in the house of Olympias, wife of King Philip, and when Aristotle was their guest at dinner I brought him his roasted meat and spiced wine, and I stood behind him with a silver bowl of lemon water so he could rinse his hands when he finished his meal. Servants are supposed to be deaf as well as mute, but I listened to him. He said that the written word was the key that would unlock the door of the storehouse that contains all power.'

Ariadne nodded. 'You make far more sense than most whom I've trained, but I must confess I find it difficult to believe you possess the talents you claim. We can solve the question by putting you to the test.' She walked to a shelf hidden behind a drape of heavy silk. 'A woman,' she said, examining the shelves piled high with books and scrolls, 'must conceal her learning, even when she utilizes it. A man resents the woman who knows too much.' Selecting a scroll, she handed it to the girl. 'Read from this,' she commanded. 'Select any passage you wish.'

There was a hint of uneasiness in Thais' eyes, but she relaxed when she opened the scroll, and after unrolling it, searched for a few moments before she began to read:

It is not strength, but art, obtains the prize,
And to be swift is less than to be wise.
'Tis more by art, than force of num'rous strokes.

Ariadne was not completely convinced. 'There are many who have memorized passages from the *Iliad*, and it might be that you recognized a few words and knew the rest by heart.'

The girl accepted the challenge immediately. 'May I select another at random?' Not waiting for a reply, she walked to the shelves and took the first scroll from the top of a thick pile. Unrolling it, she scanned it briefly, then began to read again:

Every art looks after its own interest. And its own interest is to be as much itself, and do its own work as well as is possible. And so its purpose is to do good to those on whom it is used, not to the expert in the art. The physician, as a physician, does good to those who are ill, not to himself—he only does himself good as an expert in the practise of his art. So you see, the ruler, as a ruler, does good to those under his rule. As a ruler he keeps his eyes fixed on that purpose in all he says and does.

Ariadne was impressed. 'Do you happen to know what you were reading?'

'It was Plato's dream of an ideal society, which he called the *Republic*. He was quoting Socrates.'

'I'm not sure there's much I can teach you, child. It would appear that you spent more time in the libraries of the lords of Macedon than in their kitchens. Do you play the lyre?'

Thais shook her head.

'I'm relieved,' Ariadne said dryly. 'I was beginning to fear that a paragon had found her way to my house.' Returning to her divan, she stretched out on it and, her eyes still searching, spoke gently. 'Are you a virgin?'

Thais hesitated.

'The truth, if you please. I accept no pupil who hides her private secrets from me.'

The girl clenched her fists. 'My virginity was taken from me by the son of a lord, a brute who used force to subdue me.'

'Did you enjoy the experience?'

Again Thais was reluctant to reveal her feelings, but she finally decided to speak candidly. 'When I lost my first sense of fear, I was more interested in his reaction. I felt neither pleasure nor dismay, but having learned that men place great value on the act of making love, I decided to use my body for my own profit.'

For a long time the woman was silent. 'Those who say the gods don't exist are mistaken,' she murmured at last. 'I can hear myself, twenty years ago, speaking with your voice, expressing your thoughts.'

'Then you'll accept me as a pupil?' Suddenly Thais looked like a little girl.

'Of course. Once in each generation, perhaps, the gods amuse themselves by singling out one person and endowing him with the attributes of greatness. Aphrodite looked down from Olympus, and reached into the wild hills of Macedon to touch you with her magic. You will become greater than your teacher, and will be remembered when Ariadne the Athenian has been forgotten.'

Speechless, unable to move, Thais was overcome with joy as she gazed at her benefactress.

Ariadne's manner changed, and her voice became crisp. 'But you aren't yet a renowned *hetaera*, and I was mistaken when I said there isn't much I can teach you. The first rule you must learn is to keep yourself scrupulously clean, and judging by your appearance, you haven't washed yourself in weeks. You'll spend the night soaking off the dirt, and tomorrow you'll become my pupil.'

The Banquet at Persepolis

The Persian Empire was so vast that it had three capitals, Babylon, Susa and Persepolis. After defeating the Persian armies in three great battles, conquering Egypt and founding Alexandria, Alexander turned and struck at the heart of the Empire, capturing the three capitals in quick succession. He spent the winter at Persepolis and during his stay he set fire to the superb palace of the Persian kings. Some later writers believed that he had done this during a drunken banquet, at the suggestion of Thais, to avenge the destruction of Athens by a Persian king – Xerxes – a hundred and twenty years earlier. Other ancient writers believed (as do most modern historians) that it was a deliberate act of policy to symbolize the extinction of the rule of the Persian royal family. It is however true that under the influence of wine Alexander's fiery nature led him to commit acts which he afterwards repented of – in particular he murdered one of his dearest friends in a drunken quarrel and mourned for him for three days afterwards. After the capture of Persepolis Alexander began a policy of adopting Persian royal customs in order to win the loyalty of his Persian subjects. He forced his generals to marry the daughters of Persian noblemen, and he himself married a Bactrian princess. This policy was disliked by the Macedonian nobles and led to conspiracies against him, but his soldiers adored him and would follow him anywhere – or almost: for when he led them to North West India and wanted to go still further east, they mutinied and obliged him to lead them back to Persia so that they could be dismissed and allowed to return to their homes in Greece.

The Banquet at Persepolis

The great Hall of One Hundred Columns was a testimonial to
the magnificence of Xerxes' brilliant reign. Each of the columns was a polished oak trunk, carved with scores of figures
and rubbed with light oil that made the wood glow. The pillars
supported a ceiling of overlapping leaves of silver and gold
plate, which reflected the light cast by thousands of candles.
Platters of gold and chalices of silver were spread on dozens of
tables, and the officers, Persian officials and ladies of Persepolis
reclined on mats covered with silk, which were spread out on
the tiled floor. The setting, Thais thought as she sat gracefully
on the dais of Xerxes at one end of the huge chamber, was
worthy of an infallible conqueror.

But she shared the uneasiness of Ptolemy, who was seated
on her left, and as she glanced at Alexander on her right, she
couldn't help wondering whether, at the moment, the emperor
was worthy of the setting.

Alexander, a crown of gold heavily encrusted with jewels
on his head, his fingers covered with rings and his lithe body
encased in a cloth-of-gold gown, was drunk.

His handsome face was red and bloated, his eyes were blood-

155

shot and his thirst seemed insatiable as he repeatedly ordered his cup-bearer to bring him more wine. Thais had been flattered when she had discovered that she and Ptolemy, Lord Bessus of Persia and his aristocratic wife and the provincial governor of Persepolis had been invited to share the dais. She had thought her victory more than half-won, and had gloated when she had seen Philotas and his exotic mistress relegated to a table at the far end of the hall. Now, however, she wished she could change places with Alana.

'Bow down before me!' Alexander shouted, laughing childishly.

The Persians obeyed literally, touching their foreheads to the floor, while the Macedonians and Hellenes stood resentfully and inclined their heads.

'They're such fools,' Alexander said to Thais in a conversational tone that startled her. 'Don't they know I'm simply amusing myself at their expense?'

His mood, violent one moment, detached the next, frightened her. 'You give them no choice. If anyone disobeys, you have the power to put him to death.'

'I don't feel like killing.'

'They don't know it.'

'But I might change. That's the problem, isn't it?' He smiled at her, then leaned forward and shouted again.

Thais looked at Ptolemy, who was tight-lipped.

'They make demands on me,' Alexander said, 'so it's only fair that I be given a chance to make a few in return.'

'Only you decide what is fair, Lord King,' she replied.

'You mean I sit in judgement on all men?'

'Of course.'

'Then you are mightier than Alexander, for you sit there at this moment, judging me.'

'Oh, no!'

'You lie,' he said civilly, turned away for a moment and knocked a platter of food from the hands of a servant.

Thais thought the evening would never end. She had always known that Alexander was not like other men when he was sober, and tonight, the first time she had ever seen him intoxicated, he was demonstrating that he reacted in a different way to strong spirits, too. He seemed to possess an uncanny ability to read the thoughts of others, and the wine had sharpened rather than dimmed his wits, his sensitivity, his ability to understand the motives of others. It had been humiliating to watch him laugh, silently, and to hear him say, 'How clever you are, Thais. You knew you'd appeal to every Macedonian here in that *peplos*.[1] You are Aphrodite and Hera, and I salute you.'

Her fear had increased as he had grown more irritable, more demanding, and she had seen Ptolemy exchange glances with Hephaestion, who was seated directly below the dais, when Alexander had quarrelled with Parmenio and reprimanded Cleitus the Black, a faithful phalanx commander, for allegedly failing to show him enough respect. Then he loudly ordered Philotas to remove his gold cape. He was short-tempered with servants who insisted on placing platters of food before him, he cursed his cupbearer, whom he called clumsy and slow, and Thais was afraid his anger would be turned against her because of some imagined insult.

She knew now what Ptolemy had meant when he had said that the situation had changed. Alexander himself explained, his breath heavy as he leaned on one elbow. 'I've spent my entire life working,' he told her, 'and whenever I think I'm ready to relax, to enjoy the fruits of my victories, I'm chal-

---

[1] *peplos*: part of a woman's clothing worn over another garment—something like a cross between a shawl and an Indian sari. It could be elaborate and beautiful.

lenged by a new goal. Why can't I drown myself in wine, as other men do?'

'You are unique, Lord King.'

He laughed harshly. 'Nothing dulls my mind. Last night I drank a whole skin of wine, but I could still read and write and plan and think. Two nights ago they told me I'd become ill, but I drank even more than Antigonus the Elder, and when I had sent everyone away, I studied maps and charts until daybreak. Why do I suffer from the curse of a mind that gives me no peace?'

Thais didn't dare tell him the truth, that he had driven himself unmercifully since the day he had been elected as his father's successor, and that he was suffering from exhaustion.

He caught her arm and gripped it so hard that she wanted to scream. 'You've known scores of men, so you can see inside our souls, as Aristotle dissects our minds. What sets me apart from all others?'

He would become resentful if she tried to free her arm, so she tolerated the pain until tears came to her eyes. Ptolemy had become restless, but he had been drinking only small quantities of wine and she knew he would behave discreetly. However, glancing at him, she realized he was powerless to help her.

'I demand an answer!' Alexander raised his voice, and several of his generals, sitting below the dais, pretended not to hear him, although all conversation in the vicinity had stopped.

'I don't know,' Thais said candidly. 'I've always realized you're different, but I can't explain the reasons.'

'Try.'

'You want more than anyone else has ever wanted . . .'

'Probably, but there's more than that.'

'I hadn't finished.' She was grateful when he released her arm, but resisted the impulse to rub the bruised spot. 'You'll accept only what you yourself see and hear and learn.'

'Is that all?' Alexander sounded disappointed.

Ptolemy, scarcely aware of what he was eating, cut chunks of lamb from a bone and stuffed them into his mouth.

Thais was almost as sorry for him as she was for herself. When she had imagined herself enchanting Alexander, she had always assumed he would be sober and reasonable. But she knew now that a liaison with him would be too dangerous, that she could not deal with him on ordinary human terms. The power he wielded was too vast, and, drunk or sober, his temperament was too mercurial. If she went to bed with him, he would give her gifts of great value in the morning, cast her out and dismiss her from his palace as well as from his mind. She reflected that she should have analysed him more carefully from the start, that she should have taken her clue from the emerald he had given her in Egypt.

'You haven't answered me,' Alexander said unpleasantly, handing his chalice to his cupbearer.

'I'm a woman, Lord King, not an oracle.'

'That's an evasion. The Egyptians think I am the reincarnation of Ammon-Re. The Persians of the west believe that the spirit of Marduk lives in me, and those of the east say I'm descended from Ahura, whose existence was discovered by Zoroaster, the founder of their religion.' He grinned when he saw that Bessus and the governor of Persepolis were embarrassed, but ignored both of them as he turned back to Thais. 'Obviously I can't be all three, unless Ahura, Marduk and Ammon-Re are actually the same god. Assuming they are, do you agree with my new subjects?'

'No, Lord King.' Perhaps Alexander wanted to be flattered, but Thais could not debase herself by accepting gibberish.

'Ah, then you're more inclined to the view of some of my Hellene phalanxmen that Zeus was my father?'

She saw he was taunting her, and became annoyed. 'As both of us know, Lord King, you're the son of Philip, King of Macedon, and the Lady Olympias of Epirus.'

Ptolemy nudged her, warning her to be careful.

But Alexander was pleased. 'Spoken like a true Macedonian! You see through the subterfuge of these robes.' Snatching the crown from his head, he held it before him, staring at it. Then, suddenly, he giggled. 'How they would jeer at me if they saw me wearing this in Pella.'

Ptolemy felt compelled to intervene. 'You aren't in Pella now, Alexander. You're in Persepolis, and you're going to destroy the loyalty of your Persian subjects if you treat the crown of Xerxes disrespectfully.'

Alexander accepted the advice sulkily. 'Xerxes must have had a head made of iron. My temples ache when I wear this thing for as long as half a day.'

Thais made the mistake of laughing.

Alexander caught her wrist. 'What must I do to impress you?'

'Who am I to be impressed?' she replied. 'You've created the greatest empire ever built by one general. I stand in awe of you.'

'You speak of Alexander the warrior, not Alexander the man.' He leaned his head on her bare shoulder, and the jewels of his crown cut into her flesh.

Ptolemy clenched his fists in impotent rage.

Hephaestion, who was watching the scene, shook his head.

Thais knew precisely what he meant. Neither Ptolemy nor anyone else could help her. She had invited her predicament, and only she could extricate herself from it.

'I insist,' Alexander said thickly, 'on doing something strictly for your benefit, something that will impress you as long as you live.'

'That isn't necessary.' She made a feeble attempt to retain some shreds of dignity.

'I permit no one to contradict me!' Alexander snatched an oil lamp from the table, stood and threw it with all of his strength. It struck one of the columns, and smashed, and the burning oil scorched the carving. Laughing maniacally, he reached over the shoulder of Bessus' wife, picked up another lamp and hurled it at a post. 'Burn! Burn!' he shouted.

Some of the officers at the banquet were drunk enough to follow his example, and others simply obeyed him unquestioningly. In a few moments scores of lamps were crashing into columns and candles were held close to drapes and tapestries until the fabric became ignited.

Thais' fear deepened, and in her panic she clung to Alexander's arm, hoping to dissuade him, but he was beyond reason. 'Burn!' he shouted repeatedly in a hoarse voice.

Hephaestion joined Ptolemy on the dais, and they looked at each other in helpless anguish. 'What can we do?' Hephaestion asked.

Unable to make himself heard above the the roars of drunken men and the screams of frightened women, Ptolemy leaped to the floor and tried to find a few officers sufficiently sober to control the situation. But thick fumes of oil smoke poured up toward the ceiling, a wild stampede toward the doors began, and when several of the magnificent oak columns began to burn, it was too late for anyone to curb the tragedy. Men and women ran out into the corridors, some shrieking, some laughing, and Alexander led them down the stairs, shouting inarticulately.

Thais would have broken away from him, but he caught her

around the waist, held her firmly and dragged her with him. She stumbled, tore the hem of her *peplos* and would have fallen if Alexander had released her. But he pulled her with him down to the entrance hall, seemingly determined to destroy the entire palace. He picked up a lamp from a table, hurled it at a wall and laughed madly when it smashed. Drunken officers eager to please their commander, Persians anxious to win the approval of their new master and several of the women who wanted to attract the attention of the great conqueror vied with each other in their efforts to spread the fire. Jars of oil were poured on the bases of columns and splashed against walls, candles and tapers were applied to the wood and it seemed likely that the whole building would soon be engulfed in flames.

Ptolemy and Hephaestion dashed out and summoned the troops of the *agema*, the men of the two phalanxes stationed on the palace grounds and three companies of Persian *Immortals*. Bessus joined his former enemies, and all three worked frantically to halt the fire, but Alexander, still clutching Thais, paid no attention to their efforts. He continued to laugh and shout until several enthusiasts started to rock the huge statue of Xerxes that dominated the entrance. It began to wobble on its base, and drunken men joined their comrades in ever-increasing numbers, pushing it.

Alexander, suddenly aware of the commotion, released Thais and stared at his subordinates, an expression of horror in his bleary eyes. He shouted, but no one heard him, and he raced forward, shoving Macedonian officers and Persian nobles out of his path. His hands slipped as he climbed the statue, but he clung grimly to the folds in the carved marble and did not stop until he caught hold of the statue's left elbow.

Several soldiers studied the heavy figure, and Alexander,

unmindful of the smoke that was pouring through the hall, half-concealing him from the crowd below, gestured sharply with his free hand.

Everyone halted, and for a moment there was no sound except the hissing and crackling of burning wood. 'Any man who destroys the statue of Xerxes the Great will be responsible to me,' he said and although he spoke in harsh Macedonian, even the Persians unfamiliar with the language grasped his meaning. 'He who dishonours Xerxes dishonours me.'

Several women screamed as he leaped to the floor. But he was as relaxed as a cat, and although his cumbersome robes had hindered him, he was unhurt. Apparently sober now, he spoke again, crisply and energetically. 'Send the women into the open so they won't be trampled or suffocated. Bring up two more companies of foot soldiers to fight the fires. And let every man who can carry a bucket bring water!'

Thais made no protest as a member of the *agema* shepherded her through the open doors, and down the broad steps at the front of the building, leaving her on the lawn. She held a hand over her mouth as she gazed at the inferno that had been the most handsome palace in all of Persia. The gold and silver roof of the Hall of Xerxes had melted, and yellow flames leaped up, vanished for a moment and then reappeared, reaching toward the star-filled sky. Elsewhere, smoke was pouring from the windows, and men were working frantically now, trying to control the conflagration.

Order had been established, thanks to the efforts of Ptolemy, Hephaestion and Bessus, and Macedonians and Hellenes, Persians and Kurds and Huzhas worked side by side. Four columns of troops had been formed in lines leading to the artificial lake that graced the grounds of the palace, and men passed full buckets of water from hand to hand almost as rapidly as empty pails moved in the opposite direction to be refilled. Phalanxmen and *Immortals* ripped away parts of their uniforms, tied sopping rags over their noses and mouths, and wielding double-edged attack axes, fought the fire as courageously as they had battled against each other.

Thais felt cold and frightened, and was only vaguely aware of the other women standing nearby. Alana, who had been weeping hysterically, no longer looked exotically attractive; the girl's face was smeared with streaks of kohl, her sleek hair was disarranged and she had lost one of her earrings. But it was impossible for Thais to feel any elation, and she no longer cared about her own appearance.

Convinced that her ambition had caused the needless tragedy, she believed that Alexander would not have behaved so outrageously if she had acted with greater dignity through all the preceding months. She had been obsessed by the desire to share his exalted position, but she had finally realized tonight that no woman would ever enjoy his confidence. He had inherited a trait of loneliness from Olympias, and this quality, which verged on madness, probably was the source of his inner power. It enabled him to stand apart from other men, to form no deep personal attachments, to inspire respect and admiration and devotion, but not love. Certainly he could never love anyone other than himself, and was too conscious of every move, every gesture, to think of a partner. Even while pretending to create a scene for a woman who had been trying to attract him for many months, he had been putting on a performance for the benefit of everyone in the banquet hall. Thais was herself enough of an actress to understand that much about him, and she felt sorry for any woman who became his mistress.

She knew her own limits, and wanted no more to do with him. Perhaps it was weakness to admit that his brilliance, his natural talent for treating other people as though they were inanimate objects frightened her, but she was willing to concede that he was one man she could not understand, much less control. She could never enjoy sharing his power and glory if she lived in constant fear that she might be thrown aside without reason when the cold demons that were a part of his nature came to life in him.

Ptolemy was directing a company of men breaking down a wall, and Thais smiled tremulously as she heard his hoarse, grating voice. He was ruthless and often cruel, but at least he was human; when he went into battle, she felt sure, he had to struggle to control his fears. But Alexander performed feats of valour because he didn't know the meaning of fear, and, in a sense, the Egyptians and Persians were right when they hailed him as a god.

Self-chastened, Thais watched the men extinguish the fire. It was impossible to save the wing in which the gutted Hall of Xerxes was located, but as nearly as she could judge, the flames had not caused much damage elsewhere, and she shared the relief of the Persian ladies when it became obvious that the greater portion of the palace would be saved. At least she would not have the destruction of the whole building on her conscience.

The crowd of observers parted, and Alexander, looking calm and unruffled, walked toward Thais, flanked by two members of his *agema*. 'Come with me,' he said, and, giving her no chance to reply, took her arm.

Her instinct told her that he intended to make love to her, and although this was the moment for which she had schemed and connived, the prospect sickened her. Yet she could not protest, and conscious of scores of people watching her, she accompanied the king into the palace. The odours of scorched fabrics and burned wood were still strong in the entrance chamber, but the windows of Alexander's private apartment on the second floor were open, cool night breeze had dispelled the last trace of smoke and there was a faint scent of jasmine in the air. Thais saw that a mound of flowers had been crushed in a bowl, and walking to it, she bent down and smelled the fragrance.

'I hope,' Alexander said, 'that you appreciated the spectacle. There are few women who can boast that a king destroyed a palace for their pleasure.'

The Battle off Cyprus

When Alexander died of fever at the age of thirty-three his conquests proved too immense, and his generals too unruly and ambitious for any lesser man to control. Several of the generals tried, but others always combined to oppose them, and there followed years of fighting during which the most successful established themselves as rulers (and eventually called themselves kings) in the areas of the empire which they had managed to hold. Demetrius Poliorcetes (the name means Demetrius the Besieger of Cities) was the son of one of these generals. Great good looks and a kingly presence, a fascinating personality, brilliance as a general and military engineer (besieging cities was his speciality: hence his name), daring and imagination persuaded some men that he would prove to be a second Alexander; but he lacked Alexander's single-mindedness, and success and power made him self-indulgent. Together with his father he made two bold attempts to gain control of the whole empire, and in the course of many victories and disasters he won and lost two kingdoms before his final disaster; after which he drank himself to death as the prisoner of one of his rivals. His father had been killed in battle twenty years earlier: however his son, who had none of his father's brilliance but a much more solid character, afterwards succeeded in reconquering one of Demetrius's kingdoms – Macedonia – and founded a line of kings there, the last two of which – Demetrius's great-grandson and great-great-grandson – each fought, and lost, a great war against the Romans.

An early episode in Demetrius's career was his conquest of the island of Cyprus, which was then a possession of the Ptolemy who had made himself king of Egypt. Ptolemy's forces in Cyprus were commanded by his brother Menelaus. Demetrius attacked these and drove them inside the city of Salamis which he then besieged. Before the siege lines were complete Ptolemy had set out from Egypt with a large fleet and army to drive him away. Instead of retreating, Demetrius left a few of his ships to bottle up Menelaus' fleet in the narrow harbour of Salamis and waited for Ptolemy's fleet in the open sea, where it would be impeded by having to protect the transport ships carrying the troops and baggage for the land campaign.

This is an account of the naval battle that followed.

The
Battle off
Cyprus

It was a glorious morning for a battle, clear sunshine right to the horizon which showed like a wall of blue against the paler sky. A slow swell seemed as if it would last all day, so that the rowers would not be put off their stroke by unexpected waves. There was a light onshore breeze, better than a flat calm for men who must labour to the limit of their strength; though the set of the wind meant that the lee shore of Cyprus looming high to starboard would claim crippled ships. That would make things easier for the victors, Demetrius thought to himself; he was pleased, since he was certain of victory.

From the poop of his tall sevener he could survey the disposition of his ships. They stretched to starboard in a firm well-ordered line until the right-hand squadron hugged the shore. It was unusual for the admiral to take station on the left, since in any battle the right is the post of honour; but Demetrius had a plan, an intricate and daring plan, and this was part of it.

Demetrius had decided to play double or quits. He would fight Ptolemy at sea before the Egyptian army could come to land, while the enemy were still hampered with transports and baggage. If he lost, defeat would be final; for Menelaus lay in his rear with a strong army and sixty undamaged ships. But if he beat Ptolemy he would conquer Cyprus.

To block the narrow harbour of Salamis he left ten picked warships. Only ten ships against sixty, but side by side they barred the channel and the enemy could not see that they were unsupported. 'Besides,' he said to the council of war, 'a general who has shut himself up is usually slow to come out again. Behind his walls he feels secure. He has already persuaded himself that the open country belongs to his besiegers. Menelaus will get word of our movement; at the outposts mercenaries gossip with old friends on the other side. He will recognize the chance to break out. But he won't jump at it. He likes safety. He will take more than a day to brace himself for the adventure, and one day is all we need.' With reluctance the council had agreed.

In one day he must win his victory. A drawn fight would not help him in the least. If Ptolemy was merely checked he could land his troops elsewhere in the island and still manoeuvre to raise the siege. This day's fight would be all or nothing.

He had disposed his fleet for victory or death. On his right, inshore, were his weaker ships, contingents from Asia and the islands and those rowed by hired mercenaries. The seaward left wing, which he led in person, was made up of his own picked seveners. There were seven of these in all, longer and broader and more stoutly built than any warship with lesser rowing-benches. They had been made to his own design in his own shipyards; their rowers and marines were his own faithful servants, men who had followed him since his first campaign six years ago.

Next to the seveners, the super-dreadnoughts, lay the forty ships of the Athenian navy. With four men to each oar they were just strong enough to lie in the line of battle. The shipwrights of Piraeus could have built seveners or even something larger; but Demetrius wished to employ all his excellent Athenian sailors, and fourers could be turned out in quantity during the single winter that Athens had been free. It was curious that independent Athenian democrats, men who would not work as foremen or bailiffs or in any other job that entailed obeying orders all the time, jumped at the chance to row in a galley. It was about the hardest work ever demanded of a man, so hard that the Carthaginians were said to use chained slaves as rowers; but in Athens it was considered honourable, and more fitting for a democrat than fighting on land. For only a man of some means could fit himself out with the complete panoply of a spearman. Athenians were proud of their seamanship; once afloat they obeyed orders without answering back. An Athenian fourer, manned by volunteers, could face any fiver rowed by Ptolemy's hirelings.

The Egyptians were quite close before he could see them in detail. Warships with their masts struck in readiness for battle did not show clearly against the heaving sea. But an experienced look-out could count ships by their oar-foam before he could clearly discern their hulls; Demetrius knew that he faced Ptolemy's 140 ships, without detachments. He himself had in line only 108, since ten of his best vessels were bottling up Menelaus.

In the enemy fleet there was only one sevener. Most of their ships were fivers, as might be expected; but among the nearest on the hostile right wing, were a few obsolete three-ers and some clumsy hulks which might be oared transports hastily modified for battle. Demetrius whistled with joy. He had been surprised by the reports of his spies, though he believed them; it had seemed unlikely that Ptolemy, with neither ship-timber nor trained sailors to be found in his kingdom, could send to sea as many as 200 warships. Now it was explained. Ptolemy had added to the paper strength of his fleet by bringing in vessels unfit for modern war. This was going to be easier than he had feared.

Best of all, Ptolemy had drawn up his line exactly as Demetrius had hoped. That solitary sevener must be the flagship; it lay in the middle of the fleet, with the weaker auxiliaries far out on the wings. Ptolemy planned to attack in the centre, as though he were fighting in the open sea; he had forgotten that menacing lee shore on his left.

Everywhere trumpets sounded. Flutes trilled as the rowers changed from paddling to the fast battle-stroke. Demetrius heard his shipmaster mutter, 'In, out,' and thump the gunwale to give out the time to the flagship's flute. The great sevener began to draw ahead of the Athenian fourers.

Demetrius turned to the officers on the poop behind him.

'Remember, gentlemen, no boarding before I set the example. Of course we shall sink the first ship we ram; I'd be ashamed of you all if we didn't. But we are fighting against odds, and we must sink three or four before we think of booty. Whoops, there goes the first arrow! We're off! Shields up, and stand firm for the bump!'

He began to sing a nonsensical nursery rhyme. This was the supreme joy that life had to offer. He was going to bowl over these enemies, smash them, make them turn tail. They would try to kill him; but they couldn't, because he was a better man than any of them. All the same, he was risking his life, and could there be a more pleasurable gamble? He would win, because he was Demetrius son of Antigonus. All the thousands of men in his fleet had confidence in him. And Ptolemy's thousands had rowed a long journey to furnish this pleasure. How good of them to come to meet him! What a pity so many of them would be drowned. A battle was the best pastime imaginable, but it would be better still if no one were killed.

But then no one could display his courage. Anyway, here was this splendid battle, specially arranged for his enjoyment. He would enjoy it.

The bump came; a hard bump, because the shipmaster had taken advantage of his admiral's ecstasy to run against a weak adversary. He met the little three-er squarely, beak to beak, instead of trying to sheer off a line of oars by a glancing blow. The flagship shuddered, and some marines fell flat on her deck. But the beak of the little Egyptian was driven back right through her bow-planking, so that she drifted away a waterlogged and unmanageable wreck.

'A bigger one next time,' shouted Demetrius. 'Come on, boys, get rowing again. Master, hard astarboard. Pull on that steering-oar. Don't row through their line, row down it. Hoist the signal "Follow the admiral" so that the other seveners turn with us.'

He had come out of his trance. He was alive all over his body. He could see and hear everything that happened in every part of the action, right up to the Cyprian shore. In the centre the island contingent bore up very creditably under Ptolemy's attack. Fine seamen, those islanders; they had lost some oars smashed, but so had the Egyptians. By clever steering they had avoided a head-on crash and the two lines of battle were locked together. Close inshore his weakest squadron had been driven back, but they were still fighting and none of their ships had been completely disabled.

The seveners on his immediate right had smashed through the enemy line with him; beyond them the Athenians held their own against bigger fivers. Everything was going according to plan.

Once the flagship had speed on her he rolled up the Egyptian right. His shipmaster caught a fiver broadside on, so that the beak cut her nearly in half. As her crew jumped overboard

Demetrius remembered to tell his marines not to shoot arrows at men struggling in the water.

The Egyptians backed water, turning to form a defensive flank. It was the only sensible thing to do; but ships going astern, with the steering-oar hard over, move terribly slowly. The flagship caught another fiver, shearing off all her starboard oars. Three ships wrecked, and not a scratch on his own crew. This was life as a god should live it.

Ptolemy's men did not panic. The worst of them were honest mercenaries who gave value for money, and they were stiffened by devoted retainers who had served their leader since Alexander died in Babylon. They kept the beaks of their ships towards the foe, striving continually to restore their shattered line. But now there was a lee shore behind them. Inexorably they were driven towards it.

By midday the rowers on both sides were too exhausted for further ramming. The ships barely moved, jostling beak to beak. This was the time to board. Demetrius jumped from the bows of his flagship to the foredeck of an enemy fiver. His staff and marines, even some of his rowers, swarmed after him. In a few minutes the fiver was won, but Demetrius did not himself board another. In those few minutes he had seen rowers cut down at the oars, men stabbed in the throat as they cried for mercy, fugitives run through the back. It was not the kind of fighting that gave him pleasure. Returned to his flagship, he gave the order to back water, clear of the mêlée; during the rest of the action his ship moved up and down the line, occasionally boring in to lend her great weight where it was needed.

The sun was still high when Ptolemy admitted defeat. The great Egyptian flagship, the only sevener in their fleet, had also retired from the fighting line. Suddenly she charged, shearing off the oars of two Athenian fourers who tried gallantly to intercept her. A gap showed in Demetrius's line, and other Egyptian ships streamed through it. But they did not come about to take their foes in the rear; they limped off westward at the best speed of their exhausted rowers. After a score of Egyptians had got through the Athenians closed the gap; and the remainder of the enemy, hemmed close against the rocks of Cyprus, cocked their oars in token of surrender.

Too weary to stand, drenched with sweat and spray, Demetrius crouched in his folding chair. He could see that his men were accepting the surrender of all who sought quarter, as was natural when mercenary fought mercenary. There seemed nothing more for him to do. He was about to give orders to make for the shore when he felt the flagship turn under him as the flute struck up the battle-stroke. He sprang to his feet, looking round for this new danger.

'What's up?' he called to the shipmaster. 'The battle's won, isn't it? Haven't the men done enough for today?'

'The fighting is over, my lord god,' answered the sailor, 'but the day's work isn't. If it's a question of gathering booty the men have one more spurt left in them. Look beyond that headland. Can you see masts showing? It's Ptolemy's transports and baggage, sailing ships all of them; and they are stuck in the bay with the wind foul for Egypt. Our lads want to pick up what's due to them before the mud-crushers come from the siege-lines and steal it all. I've heard that Ptolemy uses a silver chamber-pot at home in Alexandria. I wonder does he take it to war with him?'

'I expect so. I brought mine, though it's gold, not silver. But I am a Saviour God and Ptolemy's only a Pharaoh. Silly of me to forget the spoil. I enjoy fighting so much that sometimes I forget what we are fighting for.'

'You fought for the world, my lord god, and you have won it. All the same, I would like a silver chamber-pot. Permission to proceed, sir?' When asking for orders a veteran shipmaster omitted divine attributes.

While the flagship led the fleet to plunder, Demetrius sat in his chair in a weary stupor. Through his head ran the wonderful phrase: 'I fought for the world and I have won it.'

The Sybil

Prophecies, and other ways of foretelling the future, were taken far more seriously by the Greeks and Romans than they are today. Although we may enjoy reading our 'stars' in the papers, and even feel a bit superstitious about what 'they' say will happen to us, it is not part of our religion, and we do not go miles to consult a priestess about what is in store for us, and then believe her every word.

But this is what the Greeks used to do with the words of the priestess at Delphi – which place became so important in people's minds that it was called 'the navel of the earth'. The priestess had several names; in this book she is called a 'pythia', and the Romans called her a sybil.

In Pär Lagerkvist's book, *The Sybil*, one of the Delphic priestesses tells her life. This passage describes how she, a simple peasant girl, was chosen to be the priestess, and what it meant for her and her family.

The Sybil

As I grew up it began to be noticed that I was not quite like other girls of my age. I saw visions and heard voices; this was when the signs of womanhood first appeared. Later it passed. Yet I was still abstracted and alien to reality in some way; I began to keep even more to myself than before, and ceased to confide in mother. I felt my loneliness and my difference from other people more keenly. I could not explain it, but it caused me suffering. And I grew very restless; I felt unsafe, though I was in the midst of safety. That very security began to disturb and oppress me. It was queer: I liked to feel it all about me—indeed I could not do without it—yet it gave me great distress. Unknown to the others, I became a stranger to their world, though I lived in it and could have lived nowhere else. What other world had I? None. My parents were the only people who existed for me and I loved them infinitely. Yet I went about my home like a stranger, filled with an unease of which they had no inkling and which, if they had, they would not have understood. They lived on in their simple faith in all about them and in a god who existed in everything that surrounded them.

God? Had I a god any longer? Yes, surely—but where was

he? He was so far away, he must have forsaken me. Or had I
forsaken him? Had I? Was that it? Why else was I so restless,
so bereft of safety? Was not god that very safety—peace and
safety? Was he not all the things I no longer possessed?

I had long spells of utter indifference. And yet I burned
with a vague longing for I knew not what. And suddenly,
without warning and for no reason at all, I would be filled with
a glowing wave—a wave of happiness and excitement which
at first was glorious, but afterwards became so violent and hot
that it filled me with anguish and terror, so that I had to press
my hand hard against my eyes for a while, until the wave
subsided and I became myself again. Myself? But who was
that?

Who was I?

All this time I was physically sound and healthy, strong and
powerfully built like my parents. That was the curious thing.
I was a blend of disease and perfect health, of an overstrung
creature and an ordinary peasant girl. For this reason my true
state was not as noticeable as one might have expected.

In time, of course, it became known that I was a little odd,
as indeed all our family were reputed to be. This must have
been what made the temple-people think of me when they
needed a new pythia. I don't remember clearly, but I believe
I was about twenty when this happened. Those who ruled and
ordained made up their minds that this poor, odd peasant girl
who was thought to be rather simple, and whose parents
were dependent on the temple and on god, would do very well.
Also she came of a pious and very god-fearing home, they had
heard, and this was a good thing.

Father and mother were quite bewildered when the pro-
posal was made to them. They had never imagined such a
thing. They realized that it was a great honour—for it was, of
course; it was certainly that. And they knew that the god

was a great and mighty god who had an incomparable dwelling-place: a temple which they must say was very fine and splendid, though they had only been inside it a few times and had felt quite lost there among all the precious things and strange people. Nor could one well refuse the mighty ones up there, the most powerful in all Delphi. Whatever such men proposed must be right. Though one didn't understand enough about it to know how to answer. They supposed they would have to say yes—to trust in god and hope it was he who wished it, anxious though it made them to hand me over to something they knew nothing whatever about.

And I? myself?

I was strangely troubled when I heard of it. Chosen? Was I chosen? Summoned to the temple? To god?

Chosen to be his instrument, to speak his words—words inspired by him—I to be filled with his spirit, seized by holy rapture?

I? I chosen for this?

It aroused a tumult in me; it frightened me, annihilated me —and filled me with boundless happiness.

Was it possible? Could *I* be wanted by god? But they said so, they believed so. By god, who had forsaken me. Whom I had forsaken. Could such a thing come about? Was I chosen by him to be his handmaid, his prophetess, would he speak through *my* mouth? It was inconceivable—a miracle. Was it the miracle I had been awaiting?

No, god had not forgotten me, not forsaken me; nor I him— no, that never. He called me and I came; I came with my whole heart already filled with him.

God was calling me!

When the first feverish excitement had passed I went about in quiet joy, thinking only of the wonder that awaited me. Now I should know peace and security again, with him.

181

Mother and I were to go up to the temple together. We went one morning, and when we had made known our errand we were shown into a house by the temple court, and taken before the man who at that time held the highest priestly office. This was an elderly man, a member of one of the foremost families in Delphi, and we had never met such a person before. He was kind, and it was really not at all difficult. He asked a few questions about our way of life and then talked to me for a time, asking me about my childhood and other things which I couldn't think why he should want to know about; and he seemed satisfied with my presumably artless replies. At last he told me that the god dwelling in this temple was the god of light, that he was the greatest of all gods and his oracle the most eminent of any in the world. To be its priestess, called and initiated by the god himself, was a signal grace and a great responsibility. I stared down at the floor with my mind in a turmoil and full of happiness.

Then he summoned a servant, who led us across the open court into the temple, and there handed us over to a priest who was now to take charge of us.

I had never been in the temple before. And while mother stood there, simple and foreign to it all like any country woman, without looking about her very much, I gazed round enraptured, overwhelmed by the wealth and magnificence of this holy room. I had never seen anything like it before, and could never even have imagined its existence. I was seized with reverence and joy to be standing here in the presence of the divine. Yes, this was indeed the temple of the god of light, the god's own abode, the house in which he dwelt.

The priest seemed pleased with my delight and also, it seemed, because strangely enough I had never been in there before. He let me stand undisturbed in my adoration. Then he led us further into the sanctuary, to its very heart. A narrow door led into another room, and here he told mother to stay outside and wait for us. We entered the room, which was not very large, and he told me that this was where the pilgrims assembled—those who came to consult the oracle. Then we went down a narrow stairway into an almost completely dark room, lit only by two feeble oil-lamps. The air here was oppressive and musty, almost suffocating, and I felt I could hardly breathe. The floor was uneven and slimy and I realized that it was the wet, living rock itself. In it there was a crevice, over which stood a tall tripod flanked by two high bowls; or so I thought, but I couldn't discern anything clearly. And I saw no walls; the place was just a sort of pit in the ground, full of queer smells—a sickly blend of fragrance and stifling fumes that seemed to be rising from the rift in the rock and, much to my surprise, a faint, sour smell of goat. I was shaken; I breathed shallowly, panting, and once I almost thought I was going to faint.

The priest who, despite the darkness, seemed to be observing me closely, explained that this was the holy of holies where god spoke, where he inspired the pythia with what she should utter in her delirium; it was here that he would fill me with his spirit. I panted and could not answer. He seemed satisfied with me and with the impression the holy room had made upon my sensitive mind. And when he had forbidden me ever to hint at anything I had seen or might see, we turned back again. With my hand pressed hard against my eyes, as my way was when disturbed. I followed him up the narrow stair.

Mother seemed to have been waiting for us with some uneasiness, and she looked at me searchingly when I rejoined her. I was still breathing heavily, but hoped she wouldn't notice it. I looked about me with empty eyes in that great bright temple where the sunshine was pouring in exactly as before. But I felt no gladness now. And for a time, as if too full of something else, I closed my eyes against the light. It was as if for the first time I had sensed something of god.

We parted from the priest in the entrance-hall. He told me when to come again, and mother and I went home in silence, side by side. She asked what he had shown me, but I answered evasively, and we went the whole way home without another word.

I had to be alone with this as with everything else; with the knowledge that god was incomprehensible, inconceivable—that he dwelt in a hole in the ground—that he frightened me! And yet that I longed for him. For I did, I did in spite of everything, and although he was not at all as I had expected, and would hardly help me as I had thought he would. Though he was only calling me.

Why me? Why should I of all people be the chosen one?

He had a temple up in the daylight too, it was true. A beautiful, glorious temple. But from what they told me it was not the holiest place, and it was not there that I was to serve him. It was not there that he was waiting to fill me with his spirit. There he was another being and had no use for me. For it was not with his light that he meant to fill my soul. Down in a hole beneath the sanctuary he would reveal himself to me, and I would be possessed by god.

And yet—I longed to be there! Despite my fears, my terror of what awaited me, I longed only to be there! I thought of nothing else, never of anything but of being shut into that musty, stifling, suffocating hole, to prophesy with wide-open mouth, to shriek out wild, incomprehensible words through frothing lips, filled with his spirit; to be used, made use of by my god!

In this excitement I waited for what was to come. But in time the excitement subsided and was followed by a kind of lethargy in which I lived and moved; inwardly I was seething still, though the tumult never broke out. I don't know if those who now took charge of me noticed this— noticed my condition. I was often up there, for the feast-day upon which I was to become pythia was approaching and they wanted to prepare me for my task and keep me under their influence, away from my parents. I grasped little of these preparations, and in some I could see no purpose at all; some years had passed, I remember, before I understood that some nasty thing they did to me was to find out whether I was a virgin. I lived in another world than theirs; perhaps god had plunged me into this lethargy to protect me, to keep me living in his world and not in theirs. It is possible, though I know nothing about it.

The seventh day of the spring month, which is god's day, was drawing near, and it was then that I was to be pythia for the first time. I was the only one they could turn to, for the woman who had been pythia before me had died quite suddenly some time earlier, in circumstances which they did not want known. They were expecting many pilgrims to come for the festival, which lasted several days, and they were uneasy about my performance, since I had never done it before— about whether god would speak through me and whether I could endure the intense strain for so many days on end. They were full of consideration and care. But not on my account; I realized that even then, though I was like a child and had hardly ever been out among people before and knew almost nothing about them. I understood too that they lived not for god but for his temple—that it was the temple they loved and not him—and for its prestige and renown in the world. Great flocks of pilgrims would certainly be coming to this god's most solemn festival as usual, bringing the temple many gifts which would still further increase its wealth and power. All the inns were expected to be full and everyone in the city would profit in one way or another by what was to take place. These feasts which brought visitors from all over the world meant much to the people here; indeed it was by them they lived. The whole city was preparing to receive the guests.

I didn't understand this then; I knew nothing about it, but later I was to know it all too well. I was to learn what manner of thing surrounded god and his holy place and what his fame meant to the people in all these houses that clung to the mountain round about the temple like a swarming ant-hill. Because of their association with god and because they did no mundane work, they considered themselves to be in a privileged position, and in fact looked down upon the strangers who made their way to this remarkable community in the mountains. They were very proud of their city and regarded it as holy, because everyone in it lived on god.

But all this was still hidden from me; I noticed a great commotion but gave it no thought, and in a way did not see it. I went about in my daze, into which god himself had perhaps plunged me, seemingly untouched by anything outside.

The day came, god's day, with which his festival opened, and I remember that morning very well. Never was there such a sunrise over these mountains—never, at least, that I have seen. I had fasted for three days and was light, weightless as a bird. I bathed in Castalia's spring; the water was fresh and I felt pure—freed from all that did not belong to god's morning. They dressed me as a bride—his bride—and I walked slowly along the sacred way to the temple. People must have been massed all along the wayside and in the open court itself, but I never noticed them or knew that they were there. I existed only for god. And I walked up the steps of the temple where one of his servants sprinkled me with holy water, and stepped into his radiant sanctuary, into all the brightness where he was not waiting for me, where I might not serve him. I walked through it with the tears burning under my closed eyelids—for I shut my eyes not to see his glory and perhaps fail him—fail in the task which he had given me to do and for which he had chosen me. Led between two priests, I passed the altar where his eternal fire was burning, entered the pilgrim's hall and went down the narrow, dim stairway into the holy of holies.

There was as little light there as before, and it was some time before I could make anything out. But I noticed the stifling fumes from the cleft at once, and they seemed even more stifling and swooning than before. I smelt the stench of goat too, but this time it was much stronger and more pungent. I could not explain it. There must have been something burning there, for I could smell that as well. And then after a while I saw a glow in a bowl in the darkness, and a little man was crouching over it, fanning life into the embers with a bird's wing that looked like a kite's. A yellow-grey snake writhed past his foot and vanished swiftly in the darkness. This filled me with terror, for I had heard it whispered that the former pythia died from the bite of such a snake, but I had not believed it, and I had seen no snakes when I was there before. Later I learned that it was true; that they were always there and were much venerated, because they were oracle-beasts and had divine percipience. I also learned that the embers glowing in the bowl were pieces of laurel-wood, which was the god's sacred tree and whose smoke the priestess must inhale to be filled with his spirit.

Now the little man rose up from his bowl and his bird's wing and looked at me so kindly that my terrors were a little allayed. His dry, wizened face was good-natured, and he even smiled at me a little. I didn't know then that he was to be my only friend in the sanctuary, my help and consolation through the years, and especially when fate swooped down upon me like an eagle from its cleft. In my present drowsy state I took little note of him, but I felt that he was not like the others and that he meant me nothing but good, although he had to attend to his work here. It was he who now handed me a bowl of fresh laurel-leaves, recently plucked in the god's sacred grove; these I must chew, together with ashes, for this too would fill me with his spirit. And it was then that the little servant of the oracle smiled at me, as if to calm my fears, and amongst all these frightening things his smile was kind and reassuring. But of course he said nothing to me, for here in the holiest place no one might speak.

What he gave me tasted horrible; and whether because of its effect on me or because of my exhaustion after fasting, I felt ill, and reeled a little. The two priests of the oracle who were watching me the whole time helped me up on to the tripod, which was too high for me to mount unaided; then they set the dish of embers on a high stand, bringing it to a level with my head, and with every breath I had to inhale the drugging smoke. It was acrid, and produced a peculiar giddiness. But it was the fumes rising from the cleft in the rock that affected me most, for I was far more aware of them now that I was sitting directly over them: they were poisonous and nauseous. It was horrible, and the thought flashed through my mind that the cleft was believed by some to run right down into the realms of death, from which the oracle really drew its power; for death knows all things. I was seized with horror at having this beneath me, horror of losing consciousness and perhaps sinking and being engulfed in it—horror of the realms of death . . . the realms of death. . . . I felt myself sinking, sinking. . . . But where was god, where was god! He was not there, he was not coming to me. He did not fill me with his spirit as he had promised. I was only sinking, sinking. . . .

With my senses quite clouded, half-conscious, I dimly saw one of the priests of the oracle leading forward from the obscurity a he-goat with unusually large horns; it seemed to me that he poured water over its head. Then I knew no more.

But all at once everything changed. I felt relief, release; a feeling not of death but of life, life—an indescribable feeling of delight, but so violent, so unprecedented. . . . It was he! He! It was he who filled me, I felt it, I knew it! He was filling me, he was annihilating me and filling me utterly with himself, with his happiness, his joy, his rapture. Ah, it was wonderful to feel his spirit, his inspiration coming upon me—to be his, his alone, to be possessed by god. By his ecstasy, his happiness, by the wild joy that was in god. Is there anything more wonderful than sharing god's delight in being alive?

But the feeling mounted and mounted; it was still full of delight and joy, but it was too violent, too overpowering, it broke all bounds—it broke me, hurt me, it was immeasurable, demented—and I felt my body beginning to writhe, to writhe in agony and torment; being tossed to and fro and strangled, as if I were to be suffocated. But I was not suffocated, and instead I began to hiss forth dreadful, anguished sounds, utterly strange to me, and my lips moved without my will; it was not I who was doing this. And I heard shrieks, loud shrieks; I didn't understand them, they were quite unintelligible, yet it was I who uttered them. They issued from my gaping mouth, though they were not mine. . . . It was not myself at all, I was no longer I, I was his, his alone; it was terrible, terrible and nothing else!

How long it went on I don't know. I had no sense of time while it was happening. Nor do I know how I afterwards got out of the holy of holies or what happened next; who helped me and took care of me. I awoke in the house next to the temple where I lived during this time, and they said I had lain in a deep sleep of utter exhaustion. And they told me that the priests were much pleased with me and that I had exceeded all their hopes as priestess of the oracle. The old woman with whom I lived told me this, and then she left me to have a thorough rest.

I lay there in my bridal gown, as god's bride. It was the only bridal gown I would ever wear. And I remember feeling the fine, strange fabric, and being very lonely.

God? Who was god? And where was he now? Why was he not here? No longer with me? Where was he, my bridegroom? Why had he forsaken me?

I didn't understand him. But I longed for him. No, I didn't understand him at all, I didn't know at all who he was—less than ever since I had been his, since he had filled me with his spirit, with his bliss, his rapture, until I screamed with pain. Yes, he had filled me with agony. Nevertheless I longed for him, and him only. For without him all was nothingness and void.

Suppose he were to come here to me from his temple, where no doubt he was now being worshipped by his people, by all those who adored him there for his glory's sake! If he were to come and take me in his arms, as lovers surely do, afterwards. Not let me lie here quite alone in my bridal gown, as if forsaken by him, by my beloved, now that he had no further use for me—now that I had fulfilled my task, and to his satisfaction. Now that the fever, the delirium, the possession was over. Why did he love me only then? Why was he with me only then?

How gladly I would have rested quite still in his embrace, without raving or any excitement. Just rested safely and happily in his arms.

No, I did not want to be possessed by god; I wanted him to love me as he loved others, and give me security and peace thereby. Only peace and security in his embrace.

Or did I not want this? Was this not what I longed for?

It was, it was. But should I ever experience it? Was I meant for that—was it for that he wanted to use me?

Security. Peace. How could I desire such things? How could I believe I could find such things in his embrace? How could I ask security of god?

God could not be as I wished him to be, as I so much wanted him to be. He could not. God was not security and repose and rest. He was unrest, conflict and uncertainty. Those things were god.

I lay and watched dusk darkening in the room. He had plunged me into so deep a sleep that it was now evening—the day was over.

In the morning, early in the morning, as soon as the sun rose above the mountains, my bridegroom would come to me, he would fill me again with his spirit, his hot breath, his bliss, and I should be his once more!

So began my life as his priestess—my long service with him.